The Annals ... ... Poor

by

Legh Richmond

The Echo Library 2007

Published by

The Echo Library

Echo Library
131 High St.
Teddington
Middlesex TW11 8HH

www.echo-library.com

Please report serious faults in the text to complaints@echo-library.com

ISBN 978-1-40683-898-5

THE DAIRYMAN'S DAUGHTER.

PART I.

It is a delightful employment to discover and trace the operations of divine grace, as they are manifested in the dispositions and lives of God's real children. It is peculiarly gratifying to observe how frequently among the poorer classes of mankind the sunshine of mercy beams upon the heart, and bears witness to the image of Christ which the Spirit of God has impressed thereupon. Among such, the sincerity and simplicity of the Christian character appear unencumbered by those obstacles to spirituality of mind and conversation which too often prove a great hindrance to those who live in the higher ranks. Many are the difficulties which riches, worldly consequence, high connections, and the luxuriant refinements of polished society, throw in the way of religious profession. Happy indeed it is (and some such happy instances I know) where grace has so strikingly supported its conflict with natural pride, self-importance, the allurements of luxury, ease, and worldly opinion, that the noble and mighty appear adorned with genuine poverty of spirit, self-denial, humble-mindedness, and deep spirituality of heart.

But, in general, if we want to see religion in its most simple and pure character, we must look for it among the poor of this world who are rich in faith. How often is the poor man's cottage the palace of God! Many can truly declare that they have there learned the most valuable lessons of faith and hope, and there witnessed the most striking demonstrations of the wisdom, power, and goodness of God.

The character which the present narrative is designed to introduce to the notice of my readers is given *from real life and circumstances*. I first became acquainted with her by receiving the following letter, which I transcribe from the original now before me:—

"REV. SIR,

"I take the liberty to write to you. Pray excuse me, for I have never spoken to you. But I once heard you, when you preached at — Church. I believe you are a faithful preacher to warn sinners to flee from the wrath that will be revealed against all those that live in sin, and die impenitent. Pray go on in the strength of the Lord. And may he bless you, and crown your labour of love with success, and give you souls for your hire!

"The Lord has promised to be with those whom he calls and sends forth to preach his word, to the end of time; for without him we can do nothing. I was much rejoiced to hear of those marks of love and affection to that poor soldier of the S. D. militia. Surely the love of Christ sent you to that poor man. May that love ever dwell richly in you by faith! May it constrain you to seek the wandering souls of men with the fervent desire to spend and be spent for his glory! May the unction of the Holy Spirit attend the word spoken by you with power, and convey deep conviction to the hearts of your hearers! May many of them experience the divine change of being made new creatures in Christ!

"Sir, be fervent in prayer with God for the conversion of sinners. His power is great, and who can withstand it? He has promised to answer the prayer of faith, that is put up in his Son's name. 'Ask what ye will, it shall be granted you.' How this should strengthen our faith, when we are taught by the word and the Spirit how to pray! Oh, that sweet inspiring hope! how it lifts up the fainting spirits, when we look over the precious promises of God! What a mercy if we know Christ and the power of his resurrection in our own hearts! Through faith in Christ we rejoice in hope, and look up in expectation of that time drawing near when all shall know and fear the Lord, and when a nation shall be born in a day.

"What a happy time when Christ's kingdom shall come! Then shall 'his will be done on earth as it is in heaven.' Men shall be daily fed with the manna of his love, and delight themselves with the Lord all the day long. Then what a paradise below they will enjoy! How it animates and enlivens my soul with vigour to pursue the ways of God, that I may even now bear some humble part in giving glory to God and the Lamb!

"Sir, I began to write this on Sunday, being detained from attending on public worship. My dear and only sister, living as a servant with Mrs. ——, was so ill, that I came here to attend in her place and on her. But now she is no more.

"I was going to entreat you to write to her in answer to this, she being convinced of the evil of her past life, and that she had not walked in the ways of God, nor sought to please him. But she earnestly desired to do so. This makes me have a comfortable hope that she is gone to glory, and that she is now joining in sweet concert with the angelic host in heaven to sing the wonders of redeeming love. I hope I may now write, 'Blessed are the dead that die in the Lord.'

"She expressed a desire to receive the Lord's Supper, and commemorate his precious death and sufferings. I told her as well as I was able what it was to receive Christ into her heart; but as her weakness of body increased, she did not mention it again. She seemed quite resigned before she died. I do hope she is gone from a world of death and sin to be with God for ever.

"Sir, I hope you will not be offended with me, a poor ignorant person, to take such a liberty as to write to you. But I trust, as you are called to instruct sinners in the ways of God, you will bear with me, and be so kind to answer this ill-wrote letter, and give me some instruction. It is my heart's desire to have the mind that was in Christ, that when I awake up in his likeness then I may be satisfied.

"My sister expressed a wish that you might bury her. The minister of our parish, whither she will be carried, cannot come. She will lie at ——. She died on Tuesday morning, and will be buried on Friday or Saturday (whichever is most convenient to you), at three o'clock in the afternoon. Please to send an answer by the bearer, to let me know whether you can comply with this request

"From your unworthy servant,
"ELIZABETH W—."

I was much struck with the simple and earnest strain of devotion which this letter breathed. It was but indifferently written and spelt. But this the rather tended to endear the hitherto unknown writer, as it seemed characteristic of the union of humbleness of station with eminence of piety. I felt quite thankful that I was favoured with a correspondent of this description; the more so, as such characters were at that time very rare in the neighbourhood. I have often wished that epistolary intercourse of this kind were more encouraged and practised among us. I have the greatest reason to speak well of its effects both on myself and others. Communication by letter as well as by conversation with the pious poor has often been the instrument of animating and reviving my own heart in the midst of duty, and of giving me the most profitable information for the general conduct of the ministerial office.

As soon as the letter was read I inquired who was the bearer of it.

"He is waiting at the outside of the gate, sir," was the reply.

I went out to speak him, and saw a venerable old man, whose long hoary hair and deeply wrinkled countenance commanded more than common respect. He was resting his arm upon the gate, and tears were streaming down his cheeks. On my approach he made a low bow, and said,—

"Sir, I have brought you a letter from my daughter, but I fear you will think us very bold in asking you to take so much trouble."

"By no means," I replied; "I shall be truly glad to oblige you and any of your family in this matter, provided it be quite agreeable to the minister of your parish."

"Sir, he told me yesterday that he should be very glad if I could procure some gentleman to come and bury my poor child for him, as he lives five miles off, and has particular business on that day; so when I told my daughter, she asked me to come to you, sir, and bring that letter, which would explain the matter."

I desired him to come into the house, and then said,—

"What is your occupation?"

"Sir, I have lived most of my days in a little cottage at —, six miles from here. I have rented a few acres of ground, and kept some cows, which, in addition to my day-labour, has been the means of supporting and bringing up my family."

"What family have you?"

"A wife, now getting very aged and helpless; two sons, and one daughter; for my other poor dear child is just departed out of this wicked world."

"I hope for a better."

"I hope so too. Poor thing, she did not use to take to such good ways as her sister; but I do believe that her sister's manner of talking with her before she died was the means of saving her soul. What a mercy it is to have such a child as mine is! I never thought about my own soul seriously till she, poor girl, begged me to flee from the wrath to come."

"How old are you?"

"Near seventy, and my wife is older. We are getting old, and almost past our labour, but our daughter has left a good place, where she lived in service, on purpose to come home and take care of us and our little dairy. And a dear, dutiful, affectionate girl she is."

"Was she always so?"

"No, sir; when she was very young she was all for the world, and pleasure, and dress, and company. Indeed we were all very ignorant, and thought if we took care for this life, and wronged nobody, we should be sure to go to heaven at last. My daughters were both wilful, and, like ourselves, strangers to the ways of God and the word of his grace. But the eldest of them went out to service, and some years ago she heard a sermon, preached at — church by a gentleman that was going to — as chaplain to the colony, and from that time she seemed quite another creature. She began to read the Bible, and became sober and steady. The first time she returned home afterwards to see us she brought us a guinea, which she had saved from her wages, and said, as we were getting old, she was sure we should want help, adding, that she did not wish to spend it in fine clothes as she used to do, only to feed pride and vanity. She said she would rather show gratitude to her dear father and mother, because Christ had shown such mercy to her.

"We wondered to hear her talk, and took great delight in her company; for her temper and behaviour were so humble and kind, she seemed so desirous to do us good both in soul and body, and was so different from what we had ever seen her before, that careless and ignorant as we had been, we began to think there must be something real in religion, or it never could alter a person so much in a little time.

"Her youngest sister, poor soul! used to laugh and ridicule her at that time, and said her head was turned with her new ways. 'No, sister,' she would say, 'not my *head* but I hope my *heart* is turned from the love of sin to the love of God. I wish you may one day see, as I do, the danger and vanity of your present condition.'

"Her poor sister would reply, 'I do not want to hear any of your preaching; I am no worse than other people, and that is enough for me.' 'Well, sister,' Elizabeth would say, 'if you will not hear me, you cannot hinder me from praying for you, which I do with all my heart.'

"And now, sir, I believe those prayers are answered. For when her sister was taken ill, Elizabeth went to Mrs. —'s to wait in her place, and take care of her. She said a great deal to her about her soul, and the poor girl began to be so deeply affected and sensible of her past sin, and so thankful for her sister's kind behaviour, that it gave her great hopes indeed for her sake. When my wife and I went to see her as she lay sick, she told us how grieved and ashamed she was of her past life, but said she had a hope, through grace, that her dear sister's Saviour would be her Saviour too, for she saw her own sinfulness, felt her own helplessness, and only wished to cast herself upon Christ as her hope and salvation.

"And now, sir, she is gone, and I hope and think her sister's prayers for her conversion to God have been answered. The Lord grant the same for her poor father and mother's sake likewise!"

This conversation was a very pleasing commentary upon the letter which I had received, and made me anxious both to comply with the request and to become acquainted with the writer. I promised the good dairyman to attend on the Friday at the appointed hour; and after some more conversation respecting his own state of mind under the present trial, he went away.

He was a reverend old man; his furrowed cheeks, white locks, weeping eyes, bent shoulders, and feeble gait, were characteristic of the aged pilgrim. As he slowly walked onward, supported by a stick, which seemed to have been the companion of many a long year, a train of reflections occurred, which I retrace with pleasure and emotion.

At the appointed hour I arrived at the church, and after a little while was summoned to the churchyard gate to meet the funeral procession. The aged parents, the elder brother, and the sister, with other relatives, formed an affecting group. I was struck with the humble, pious, and pleasing countenance of the young woman from whom I had received the letter. It bore the marks of great seriousness without affectation, and of much serenity mingled with a glow of devotion.

A circumstance occurred during the reading of the Burial Service, which I think it right to mention as one among many testimonies of the solemn and impressive tendency of our truly evangelical Liturgy.

A man of the village, who had hitherto been of a very careless and even profligate character, went into the church through mere curiosity, and with no better purpose than that of vacantly gazing at the ceremony. He came likewise to the grave, and during the reading of those prayers which are appointed for that part of the service, his mind received a deep, serious conviction of his sin and spiritual danger. It was an impression that never wore off, but gradually ripened into the most satisfactory evidence of an entire change, of which I had many and long-continued proofs. He always referred to the Burial Service, and to some particular sentences of it, as the clearly ascertained instrument of bringing him, through grace, to the knowledge of the truth.

The day was therefore one to be remembered. Remembered let it be by those who love to hear "the short and simple annals of the poor."

Was there not a manifest and happy connection between the circumstances that providentially brought the serious and the careless to the same grave on that day together? How much do *they* lose who neglect to trace the leadings of God in providence as links in the chain of his eternal purpose of redemption and grace!

"While infidels may scoff, let us adore!"

After the service was concluded I had a short conversation with the good old couple and their daughter. She told me that she intended to remain a week or two at the gentleman's house where her sister died till another servant should arrive and take her sister's place.

"I shall be truly obliged," said she, "by an opportunity of conversing with you, either there or at my father's when I return home, which will be in the course of a fortnight at the furthest. I shall be glad to talk to you about my sister, whom you have just buried."

Her aspect and address were highly interesting. I promised to see her very soon, and then returned home, quietly reflecting on the circumstances of the funeral at which I had been engaged. I blessed the God of the poor, and prayed that the poor might become rich in faith, and the rich be made poor in spirit.

PART II.

A sweet solemnity often possesses the mind whilst retracing past intercourse with departed friends. How much is this increased when they were such as lived and died in the Lord! The remembrance of former scenes and conversations with those who, we believe, are now enjoying the uninterrupted happiness of a better world, fills the heart with pleasing sadness, and animates the soul with the hopeful anticipation of a day when the glory of the Lord shall be revealed in the assembling of all his children together, never more to be separated. Whether they were rich or poor while on earth is a matter of trifling consequence: the valuable part of their character is, that they are "kings and priests unto God;" and this is their true nobility. In the number of now departed believers, with whom I once loved to converse on the grace and glory of the kingdom of God, was the Dairyman's daughter.

About a week after the funeral, I went to visit the family at —, in whose service the younger sister had lived and died, and where Elizabeth was requested to remain for a short time in her stead.

The house was a large and venerable mansion. It stood in a beautiful valley at the foot of a high hill. It was embowered in fine woods, which were interspersed in every direction with rising, falling, and swelling grounds. The manor-house had evidently descended through a long line of ancestry, from a distant period of time. The Gothic character of its original architecture was still preserved in the latticed windows, adorned with carved divisions and pillars and stonework. Several pointed terminations also, in the construction of the roof, according to the custom of our forefathers, fully corresponded with the general features of the building.

One end of the house was entirely clothed with the thick foliage of an immense ivy, which climbed beyond customary limits, and embraced a lofty chimney up to its very summit. Such a tree seemed congenial to the walls that supported it, and conspired with the antique fashion of the place to carry imagination back to the days of our ancestors.

As I approached, I was led to reflect on the lapse of ages, and the successive generations of men, each in their turn occupying lands, houses, and domains; each in their turn also disappearing, and leaving their inheritance to be enjoyed by others. David once observed the same, and cried out, "Behold, thou hast made my days as an handbreadth, and mine age is as nothing before thee: verily every man at his best state is altogether vanity. Surely every man walketh in a vain show; surely they are disquieted in vain: he heapeth up riches, and knoweth not who shall gather them."

Happy would it be for the rich if they more frequently meditated on the uncertainty of all their possessions, and the frail nature of every earthly tenure. "Their inward thought is, that their houses shall continue for ever, and their dwelling-places to all generations: they call their lands after their own names. Nevertheless, man being in honour abideth not: he is like the beasts that perish. This their way is their folly; yet their posterity approve their sayings. Like sheep they are laid in the grave; death shall feed on them; and their beauty shall consume in the grave from their dwelling."

As I advanced to the mansion, a pleasing kind of gloom overspread the front: it was occasioned by the shade of trees, and gave a characteristic effect to the ancient fabric. I instantly recollected that death had very recently visited the house and that one of its present inhabitants was an affectionate mourner for a departed sister.

There is a solemnity in the thought of a recent death, which will associate itself with the very walls from whence we are conscious that a soul has just taken its flight to eternity.

After passing some time in conversation with the superiors of the family, in the course of which I was much gratified by hearing of the unremitted attention which the elder sister had paid to the younger during the illness of the latter, I received likewise other testimonies of the excellency of her general character and conduct in the house. I then took leave, requesting permission to see her, agreeably to the promise I had made at the funeral, not many days before.

I was shown into a parlour, where I found her alone. She was in deep mourning. She had a calmness and serenity in her countenance which exceedingly struck me, and impressed some idea of those attainments which a further acquaintance with her afterwards so much increased.

She spoke of her sister. I had the satisfaction of finding that she had given very hopeful proofs of a change of heart before she died. The prayers and earnest exhortations of Elizabeth had been blessed to a happy effect. She described what had passed with such a mixture of sisterly affection and pious dependence on the mercy of God to sinners, as convinced me that her own heart was under the influence of "pure and undefiled religion."

She requested leave occasionally to correspond with me on serious subjects, stating that she needed much instruction. She hoped I would pardon the liberty which she had taken by introducing herself to my notice. She expressed a trust that the Lord would overrule both the death of her sister and the personal acquaintance with me that resulted from it, to a present and future good, as it respected herself, and also her parents, with whom she statedly lived, and to whom she expected to return in a few days.

Finding that she was wanted in some household duty, I did not remain long with her, but left her with an assurance that I proposed to visit her parents very shortly.

"Sir," said she, "I take it very kind that you have condescended to leave the company of the rich, and converse with the poor. I wish I could have said more to you respecting my own state of mind. Perhaps I shall be better able another time. When you next visit me, instead of finding me in these noble walls, you will see me in a poor cottage. But I am happiest when there. Once more, sir, I thank you for your past kindness to me and mine, and may God in many ways bless you for it!"

I quitted the house with no small degree of satisfaction, in consequence of the new acquaintance which I had formed. I discovered traces of a cultivated as well as a spiritual mind. I felt that religious intercourse with those of low estate may be rendered eminently useful to others, whose outward station and advantages are far above their own.

How often does it appear that "God hath chosen the weak things of the world to confound the things which are mighty and base things of the world, and things which are despised, hath God chosen, and things which are not, to bring to nought things that are; that no flesh should glory in his presence!"

It was not unfrequently my custom, when my mind was filled with any interesting subject for meditation, to seek some spot where the beauties of natural prospect might help to form pleasing and useful associations. I therefore ascended gradually to the very summit of the hill adjoining the mansion where my visit had just been made. Here was placed an elevated sea-mark: it was in the form of a triangular pyramid, and built of stone. I sat down on the ground near it, and looked at the surrounding prospect, which was distinguished for beauty and magnificence. It was a lofty station, which commanded a complete circle of interesting objects to engage the spectator's attention. Southward the view was terminated by a long range of hills, at about six miles distance. They met to the westward another chain of hills, of which the one whereon I sat formed a link, and the whole together nearly encompassed a rich and fruitful valley, filled with cornfields and pastures. Through this vale winded a small river for many miles: much cattle were feeding on its banks. Here and there lesser eminences arose in the valley: some covered with wood, others with corn or grass, and a few with heath or fern. One of these little hills was distinguished by a parish church at the top, presenting a striking feature in the landscape. Another of these elevations, situated in the centre of the valley, was adorned with a venerable holly-tree, which has grown there for ages. Its singular height and wide-spreading dimensions not only render it an object of curiosity to the traveller, but of daily usefulness to the pilot, as a mark visible from the sea, whereby to direct his vessel safe into harbour. Villages, churches, country-seats, farm-houses, and cottages, were scattered over every part of the southern valley. In this direction also, at the foot of the hill where I was stationed, appeared the ancient mansion which I had just quitted, embellished with its woods, groves, and gardens.

South-eastward I saw the open ocean, bounded only by the horizon. The sun shone, and gilded the waves with a glittering light that sparkled in the most brilliant manner. More to the east, in continuation of that line of hills where I was placed, rose two downs, one beyond the other, both covered with sheep, and the sea just visible over the furthest of them, as a terminating boundary. In this point ships were seen, some sailing, others at anchor. Here the little river which watered the southern valley finished its course, and ran through meadows into the sea, in an eastward direction.

On the north the sea appeared like a noble river, varying from three to seven miles in breadth, between the banks of the opposite coast and those of the island which I inhabited. Immediately underneath me was a fine woody district of country, diversified by many pleasing objects. Distant towns were visible on the opposite shore. Numbers of ships occupied the sheltered station which this northern channel afforded them. The eye roamed with delight over an expanse of near and remote beauties, which alternately caught the observation, and which harmonized together, and produced a scene of peculiar interest.

Westward the hills followed each other, forming several intermediate and partial valleys, in a kind of undulations, like the waves of the sea; and, bending to the south, completed the boundary of the larger valley before described, to the southward of the hill on which I sat. In many instances the hills were cultivated with corn to their very summits, and seemed to defy the inclemency of the weather, which, at these heights, usually renders the ground incapable of bringing forth and ripening the crops of grain. One hill alone, the highest in elevation, and about ten miles to the south-westward, was enveloped in a cloud, which just permitted a dim and hazy sight of a signal-post, a light-house, and an ancient chantry, built on its summit.

Amidst these numerous specimens of delightful scenery I found a mount for contemplation, and here I indulged it. "How much of the natural beauties of Paradise still remain in the world, although its spiritual character has been so awfully defaced by sin! But when divine grace renews the heart of the fallen sinner, Paradise is regained, and much of its beauty restored to the soul. As this prospect is compounded of hill and dale, land and sea, woods and plains, all sweetly blended together, and relieving each other in the landscape; so do the gracious dispositions wrought in the soul produce a beauty and harmony of scene to which it was before a stranger."

I looked towards the village in the plain below, where the Dairyman's younger daughter was buried. I retraced the simple solemnities of the funeral. I connected the principles and conduct of her sister with the present probably happy state of her soul in the world of spirits, and was greatly impressed with a sense of the importance of family influence as a means of grace. "That young woman," I thought, "has been the conductor of not only a sister, but perhaps a father and mother also, to the true knowledge of God, and may, by the divine blessing, become so to others. It is a glorious occupation to win souls to Christ, and guide them out of Egyptian bondage through the wilderness into the promised Canaan. Happy are the families who are walking hand in hand together, as pilgrims, towards the heavenly country. May the number of such be daily increased?"

Casting my eye over the numerous dwellings in the vales on my right and left, I could not help thinking, "How many of their inhabitants are ignorant of the ways of God, and strangers to his grace! May this thought stimulate to activity and diligence in the cause of immortal souls! They are precious in God's sight—they ought to be so in ours."

Some pointed and affecting observations to that effect recurred to my mind as having been made by the young person with whom I had been just conversing. Her mind appeared to be much impressed with the duty of speaking and acting for God "while it is day," conscious that "the night cometh, when no man can work." Her laudable anxiety on this head was often testified to me afterwards, both by letter and conversation. What she felt herself, in respect to endeavours to do good, she happily communicated to others with whom she corresponded or conversed.

Time would not permit my continuing so long in the enjoyment of these meditations, on this lovely mount of observation, as my heart desired. On my return home I wrote a few lines to the Dairyman's daughter, chiefly dictated by the train of thought which had occupied my mind while I sat on the hill.

On the next Sunday evening I received her reply, of which the following is a transcript:—

"Sunday.
"REV. SIR,

"I am this day deprived of an opportunity of attending the house of God, to worship him. But, glory be to his name, he is not confined to time or place. I feel him present with me where I am, and his presence makes my paradise; for where he is, is heaven. I pray God that a double portion of his grace and Holy Spirit may rest upon you this day; that his blessing may attend all your faithful labours; and that you may find the truth of his word assuring us that wherever we assemble together in his name, there is he in the midst to bless every waiting soul.

"How precious are all his promises! We ought never to doubt the truth of his word. For he will never deceive us if we go on in faith, always expecting to receive what his goodness waits to give. Dear sir, I have felt it very consoling to read your kind letter to-day. I feel thankful to God for ministers in our church who love and fear his name: there it is where the people in general look for salvation; and there may they ever find it, for Jesus' sake! May his word, spoken by you, his chosen vessel of grace, be made spirit and life to their dead souls! May it come from you as an instrument in the hands of God, as sharp arrows from a strong archer, and strike a death-blow to all their sins! How I long to see the arrows of conviction fasten on the minds of those that are hearers of the word, and not doers! O sir, be ambitious for the glory of God and the salvation of souls! It will add to the lustre of your crown in glory, as well as to your present joy and peace. We should be willing to spend and be spent in his service, saying, 'Lord, may thy will be done by me on earth, even as it is by the angels in heaven.' So you may expect to see his face with joy, and say, 'Here am I, Lord, and all the souls thou hast given me.'

"It seems wonderful that we should neglect any opportunity of doing good, when there is, if it be done from love to God and his creatures, a present reward of grace, in reflecting that we are using the talents committed to our care, according to the power and ability which we receive from him. God requires not what he has not promised to give. But when we look back, and reflect that there have been opportunities in which we have neglected to take up our cross and speak and act for God, what a dejection of mind we feel! We are then justly filled with shame. Conscious of being ashamed of Christ, we cannot come with that holy boldness to a throne of grace, nor feel that free access when we make our supplications.

"We are commanded to provoke one another to love and good works; and where two are agreed together in the things of God, they may say,—

'And if our fellowship below
    In Jesus be so sweet,
What heights of rapture shall we know
    When round the throne we meet!'

"Sir, I hope Mrs. — and you are both of one heart and one mind. Then you will sweetly agree in all things that make for your present and eternal happiness. Christ sent his disciples out, not singly, but two and two, that they might comfort and help each other in those ways and works which their Lord commanded them to pursue.

"It has been my lot to have been alone the greatest part of the time that I have known the ways of God. I therefore find it such a treat to my soul when I can meet with any who love to talk of the goodness and love of God, and all his gracious dealings. What a comfortable reflection, to think of spending a whole eternity in that delightful employment! to tell to listening angels his love 'immense, unsearchable!'

"Dear sir, I thank you for your kindness and condescension in leaving those that are of high rank and birth in the world, to converse with me, who am but a servant here below. But when I consider what a high calling, what honour and dignity, God has conferred upon me, to be called his child, to be born of his Spirit, made an heir of glory, and joint heir with Christ; how humble and circumspect should I be in all my ways, as a dutiful and loving child to an affectionate and loving Father! When I seriously consider these things, it fills me with love and gratitude to God; and I do not wish for any higher station, nor envy the rich. I rather pity them, if they are not good as well as great. My blessed Lord was pleased to appear in the form of a servant, and I long to be like him.

"I did not feel in so happy a frame of conversation that day, nor yet that liberty to explain my thoughts which I sometimes do. The fault must have been all in myself; for there was nothing in you but what seemed to evidence a Christian spirit, temper, and disposition. I very much wished for an opportunity to converse with you. I feel very thankful to God that you do take up the cross, and despise the shame: if you are found faithful, you will soon sit down with him in glory.

"I have written to the Rev. Mr. —, to thank him for permitting you to perform the burial service at — over my dear departed sister, and to tell him of the kind way in which you consented to do it. I should mention that your manner of reading the service on that day had a considerable effect on the hearers.

"Pray excuse all faults, and correct my errors. I expect in a few days to return home to my parents' house. We shall rejoice to see you there.

"From your humble servant in Christ,
"E— W—."

It was impossible to view such a correspondent with indifference. I had just returned from a little cottage assembly, where, on Sunday evenings, I sometimes went to instruct a few poor families in one of the hamlets belonging to my parish. I read the letter, and closed the day with thanksgiving to God for thus enabling those who fear his name to build up each other in fear and love.

Of old time "they that feared the Lord spake often one to another; and the Lord hearkened, and heard it, and a book of remembrance was written before him for them that feared the Lord, and that thought upon his name."

That book of remembrance is not yet closed.

PART III.

The mind of man is like a moving picture, supplied with objects not only from contemplation on things present, but from the fruitful sources of recollection and anticipation.

Memory retraces past events, and restores an ideal reality to scenes which are gone by for ever. They live again in revived imagery, and we seem to hear and see with renewed emotions what we heard and saw at a former period. Successions of such recollected circumstances often form a series of welcome memorials. In religious meditations, the memory becomes a sanctified instrument of spiritual improvement.

Another part of this animated picture is furnished by the pencil of Hope. She draws encouraging prospects for the soul, by connecting the past and the present with the future. Seeing the promises afar off, she is persuaded of their truth, and embraces them as her own.

The Spirit of God gives a blessing to both these acts of the mind, and employs them in the service of religion. Every faculty of body and soul, when considered as a part of "the purchased possession" of the Saviour, assumes a new character. How powerfully does the apostle on this ground urge a plea for holy activity and watchfulness! "What! know ye not that your body is the temple of the Holy Ghost which is in you, which ye have of God, and ye are not your own? For ye are bought with a price; therefore glorify God in your body, and in your spirit, which are God's."

The Christian may derive much profit and enjoyment from the use of the memory as it concerns those transactions in which he once bore a part. In his endeavours to recall past conversations and intercourse with deceased friends, in particular, the powers of remembrance greatly improve by exercise. One revived idea produces another, till the mind is most agreeably and usefully occupied with lively and holy imaginations.

"Lulled in the countless chambers of the brain,
Our thoughts are linked by many a hidden chain.
Awake but one, and lo! what myriads rise!
Each stamps its image as the other flies.
Each, as the varied avenues of sense
Delight or sorrow to the soul dispense,
Brightens or fades; yet all, with sacred art,
Control the latent fibres of the heart."

May it please God to bless, both to the reader and the writer, this feeble attempt to recollect some of the communications which I once enjoyed in my visits to the Dairyman's dwelling.

Very soon after the receipt of the last letter, I rode for the first time to see the family at their own house. The principal part of the road lay through retired narrow lanes, beautifully overarched with groves of nut and other trees, which screened the traveller from the rays of the sun, and afforded many interesting objects for admiration, in the flowers, shrubs, and young trees, which grew upon the high banks on each side of the road. Many grotesque rocks, with little trickling streams of water occasionally breaking out of them, varied the recluse scenery, and produced a romantic and pleasing effect.

Here and there the more distant prospect beyond was observable through gaps and hollow places on the roadside. Lofty hills, with many signal- posts, obelisks, and light-houses on their summits, appeared at these intervals; rich cornfields were also visible through some of the open places; and now and then, when the road ascended a hill, the sea, with ships at various distances, was seen. But for the most part shady seclusion, and objects of a more minute and confined nature, gave a character to the journey, and invited contemplation.

How much do they lose who are strangers to serious meditation on the wonders and beauties of nature! How gloriously the God of creation shines in his works! Not a tree, or leaf, or flower, not a bird or insect, but it proclaims in glowing language, "God made me."

As I approached the village where the good old Dairyman dwelt, I observed him in a little field, driving his two cows before him towards a yard and hovel which adjoined his cottage. I advanced very near him without his observing me, for his sight was dim. On my calling out to him, he started at the sound of my voice, but with much gladness of heart welcomed me, saying, "Bless your heart, sir, I am glad you are come: we have looked for you every day this week."

The cottage door opened, and the daughter came out, followed by her aged and infirm mother. The sight of me naturally brought to recollection the grave at which we had before met. Tears of affection mingled with the smile of satisfaction with which I was received by these worthy cottagers. I dismounted and was conducted through a neat little garden, part of which was shaded by two large overspreading elm-trees, to the house. Decency and order were manifested within and without. No excuse was made here, on the score of poverty, for confusion and uncleanliness in the disposal of their little household. Everything wore the aspect of neatness and propriety. On each side of the fireplace stood an old oaken arm-chair, where the venerable parents rested their weary limbs after the day's labour was over. On a shelf in one corner lay two Bibles, with a few religious books and tracts. The little room had two windows: a lovely prospect of hills, woods, and fields, appeared through one; and the other was more than half obscured by the branches of a vine which was trained across it; between its leaves the sun shone, and cast a cheerful light over the whole place.

"This," thought I, "is a fit residence for piety, peace, and contentment. May I learn a fresh lesson for advancement in each, through the blessing of God on this visit."

"Sir," said the daughter, "we are not worthy that you should come under our roof. We take it very kind that you should travel so far to see us."

"My Master," I replied, "came a great deal further to visit us poor sinners. He left the bosom of his Father, laid aside his glory, and came down to this lower world on a visit of mercy and love; and ought not we, if we profess to follow him, to bear each other's infirmities, and go about doing good as he did?"

The old man now entered, and joined his wife and daughter in giving me a cordial welcome. Our conversation soon turned to the loss they had so lately sustained. The pious and sensible disposition of the daughter was peculiarly manifested, as well in what she said to her parents as in what she more immediately addressed to myself. I had now a further opportunity of remarking the good sense and agreeable manner which accompanied her expressions of devotedness to God, and love to Christ for the great mercies which he had bestowed upon her. During her residence in different gentlemen's families where she had been in service, she had acquired a superior behaviour and address; but sincere piety rendered her very humble and unassuming in manner and conversation. She seemed anxious to improve the opportunity of my visit to the best purpose for her own and her parents' sake; yet there was nothing of unbecoming forwardness, no self-confidence or conceitedness in her conduct. She united the firmness and solicitude of the Christian with the modesty of the female and the dutifulness of the daughter. It was impossible to be in her company and not observe how truly her temper and conversation adorned the principles which she professed.

I soon discovered how eager and how successful also she had been in her endeavours to bring her father and mother to the knowledge and experience of the truth. This is a lovely feature in the character of a young Christian. If it have pleased God, in the free dispensation of his mercy, to call the child by his grace while the parents remain still in ignorance and sin, how great is the duty incumbent on that child to do what is possible to promote the conversion of those to whom so much is owing! Happy is it when the ties of grace sanctify those of nature!

The aged couple evidently regarded and spoke of this daughter as their teacher and admonisher in divine things, while at the same time they received from her every token of filial submission and obedience, testified by continual endeavours to serve and assist them to the utmost of her power in the daily concerns of the household.

The religion of this young woman was of a highly spiritual character, and of no ordinary attainment. Her views of the divine plan in saving the sinner were clear and scriptural. She spoke much of the joys and sorrows which, in the course of her religious progress, she had experienced; but she was fully sensible that there is far more in real religion than mere occasional transition from one frame of mind and spirits to another. She believed that the experimental acquaintance of the heart with God principally consisted in so living upon Christ by faith as to aim at living like him by love. She knew that the love of God toward the sinner, and the path of duty prescribed to the sinner, are both of an unchangeable nature. In a believing dependence on the one, and an affectionate walk in the other, she sought and found "the peace of God which passeth all understanding;" for "so he giveth his beloved rest."

She had read but few books besides her Bible; but these few were excellent in their kind, and she spoke of their contents as one who knew their value. In addition to a Bible and Prayer-book, "Doddridge's Rise and Progress," "Romaine's Life, Walk, and Triumph of Faith," "Bunyan's Pilgrim," "Alleine's Alarm," "Baxter's Saint's Everlasting Rest," a hymn- book, and a few tracts, completed her library.

I observed in her countenance a pale and delicate hue, which I afterwards found to be a presage of consumption; and the idea then occurred to me that she would not live very long.

Time passed on swiftly with this interesting family, and after having partaken of some plain and wholesome refreshment, and enjoyed a few hours' conversation with them, I found it was necessary for me to return homewards. The disposition and character of the parties may be in some sort ascertained by the expressions at parting.

"God send you safe home again," said the aged mother, "and bless the day that brought you to see two poor old creatures such as we are, in our trouble and affliction. Come again, sir, come again when you can; and though I am a poor ignorant soul, and not fit to talk to such a gentleman as you, yet my dear child shall speak for me. She is the greatest comfort I have left, and I hope the good Lord will spare her to support my trembling limbs and feeble spirits, till I lie down with my other dear departed children in the grave."

"Trust to the Lord," I answered, "and remember his gracious promise: 'Even to your old age I am he; and even to hoar hairs I will carry you.'"

"I thank you, sir," said the daughter, "for your Christian kindness to me and my friends. I believe the blessing of the Lord has attended your visit, and I hope I have experienced it to be so. My dear father and mother will, I am sure, remember it; and I rejoice in the opportunity of seeing so kind a friend under this roof. My Saviour has been abundantly good to me, in plucking me as 'a brand from the burning,' and showing me the way of life and peace; and I hope it is my heart's desire to live to his glory. But I long to see these dear friends enjoy the power and comfort of religion likewise."

"I think it evident," I replied, "that the promise is fulfilled in their case: 'It shall come to pass that at evening time it shall be light."

"I believe it," she said, "and praise God for the blessed hope."

"Thank him, too, that you have been the happy instrument of bringing them to the light."

"I do, sir; yet when I think of my own unworthiness and insufficiency, I rejoice with trembling."

"Sir," said the good old man, "I am sure the Lord will reward you for this kindness. Pray for us, old as we are, and sinners as we have been, that yet he would have mercy upon us at the eleventh hour. Poor Betsy strives much for our sakes, both in body and soul: she works hard all day to save us trouble, and I fear has not strength to support all she does; and then she talks to us, and reads to us, and prays for us, that we may be saved from the wrath to come. Indeed, sir, she's a rare child to us."

"Peace be to you, and to all that belong to you!"

"Amen, and thank you, dear sir," was echoed from each tongue.

Thus we parted for that time. My returning meditations were sweet, and I hope profitable.

Many other visits were afterwards made by me to this peaceful cottage, and I always found increasing reason to thank God for the intercourse I there enjoyed.

An interval of some length occurred once during that year in which I had not seen the Dairyman's family. I was reminded of the circumstance by the receipt of the following letter:—

"REV. SIR,

"I have been expecting to see or hear from you for a considerable time. Excuse the liberty I take in sending you another letter. I have been confined to the house the greater part of the time since I left —. I took cold that day, and have been worse ever since. I walk out a little on these fine days, but seem to myself to walk very near the borders of eternity. Glory be to God, it is a very pleasing prospect before me! Though I feel the working of sin, and am abased, yet Jesus shows his mercy to be mine, and I trust that I am his. At such times—

'My soul would leave this heavy clay
    At his transporting word,
Run up with joy the shining way
    To meet and prove the Lord.

Fearless of hell and ghastly death,
    I'd break through ev'ry foe;
The wings of love and arms of faith
    Would bear me conqu'ror through.'

My desire is to live every moment to God, that I may, through his grace, be kept in that heavenly, happy frame of mind, that I shall wish for at the hour of death. We cannot live or die happy without this; and to keep it, we must be continually watching and praying: for we have many enemies to disturb our peace. I am so very weak, that now I can go nowhere to any outward means for that help which is so refreshing to my spirit.

"I should have been very happy to have heard you last Sunday, when you preached at —. I could not walk so far. I hope the word spoken by you was made a blessing to many who heard it. It was my earnest prayer to God that it might be so. But, alas! once calling does not awaken many that are in a sound sleep. Yet the voice of God is sometimes very powerful, when his ministers speak; when they are influenced by his Holy Spirit, and are simple and sincere in holding forth the word of life. Then it will teach us all things, and enlighten our mind and reveal unto us the hidden things of darkness, and give us out of that divine treasure 'things new and old.' Resting on God to work in us both to will and to do of his own good pleasure, we ought always to work as diligent servants, that know they have a good Master, that will surely not forget their labour of love.

"If we could but fix our eyes always on that crown of glory that waits us in the skies, we should never grow weary in well-doing, but should run with patience and delight in the work and ways of God, where he appoints us. We should not then, as we too frequently do, suffer these trifling objects here on earth to draw away our minds from God, to rob him of his glory and our souls of that happiness and comfort which the believer may enjoy amidst outward afflictions. If we thus lived more by faith in the Son of God, we should endeavour to stir up all whom we could to seek after God. We should tell them what he has done for us, and what he would do for them if they truly sought him. We should show them what a glorious expectation there is for all true believers and sincere seekers.

"When our minds are so fixed on God, we are more desirous of glorifying him, in making known his goodness to us, than the proud rich man is of getting honour to himself. I mourn over my own backwardness to this exercise of duty, when I think of God's willingness to save the vilest of the vile, according to the dispensations of his eternal grace and mercy. Oh, how amiable, how lovely does this make that God of love appear to poor sinners, that can view him as such! How is the soul delighted with such a contemplation! They that have much forgiven, how much they love!

"These thoughts have been much on my mind since the death of —. I trust the Lord will pardon me for neglect. I thought it was my duty to speak or write to him: you remember what I said to you respecting it. But I still delayed till a more convenient season. Oh, how I was struck when I heard the Lord had taken him so suddenly! I was filled with sorrow and shame for having neglected what I had so often resolved to do. But now the time of speaking for God to him was over. Hence we see that the Lord's time is the best time. Now the night of death was come upon him; no more work was to be done. If I had done all that lay in my power to proclaim reconciliation by Christ to his soul, whether he had heard or no, I should have been clear of his blood. But I cannot recall the time that is past, nor him from the grave. Had I known the Lord would have called him so suddenly, how diligent I should have been to warn him of his danger! But it is enough that God shows us what *we* are to do, and not what *he* is about to do with us or any of his creatures. Pray, sir, do all you can for the glory of God. The time will soon pass by, and then we shall enter that glorious rest that he hath prepared for them that love him. I pray God to fill you with that zeal and love which he only can inspire, that you may daily win souls to Christ. May he deliver you from all slavish fear of man, and give you boldness, as he did of old those that were filled with the Holy Ghost and with power!

"Remember, Christ has promised to be with all his faithful ministers to the end of time. The greater dangers and difficulties they are exposed to, the more powerful his assistance. Then, sir, let us fear none but him. I hope you will pray much for me, a poor sinner, that God will perfect his strength in my weakness of body and mind; for without him I can do nothing. But when I can experience the teaching of that Holy One, I need no other teacher. May the Lord anoint you with the same, and give you every grace of his Holy Spirit, that you may be filled with all the fulness of God; that you may know what is the height and depth, the length and breadth, of the love of God in Christ Jesus; that you may be in the hand of the Lord as a keen archer to draw the bow, while the Lord directs and fastens the arrows of conviction in the hearts of such as are under your ministry!

"I sincerely pray that you may be made a blessing to him that has taken the place of the deceased. I have heard that you are fellow-countrymen: I hope you are, however, both as strangers in this world, that have no abiding place, but seek a country out of sight.

"Pray excuse all faults.
"From your humble servant in the bonds of the gospel of Christ,
"E— W—."

When I perused this and other letters, which were at different times written to me by the Dairyman's daughter, I felt that in the person of this interesting correspondent were singularly united the characters of a humble disciple and a faithful monitor. I wished to acknowledge the goodness of God in each of these her capacities.

I sometimes entertain a hope that the last day will unfold the value of these epistolary communications, beyond even any present estimate of their spiritual importance.

PART IV.

The translation of sinners "from the power of darkness into the kingdom of God's dear Son," is the joy of Christians and the admiration of angels. Every penitent and pardoned soul is a new witness to the triumphs of the Redeemer over sin, death, and the grave. How great the change that is wrought! The child of wrath becomes a monument of grace—a brand plucked from the burning! "If any man be in Christ he is a new creature: old things are passed away; behold, all things are become new." How marvellous, how interesting, is the spiritual history of each individual believer! He is, like David, "a wonder to many," but the greatest wonder of all to himself. Others may doubt whether it be so or not; but to *him* it is unequivocally proved, that, from first to last, grace alone reigns in the work of his salvation.

The character and privileges of real Christians are beautifully described in the language of our church; which, when speaking of the objects of divine favour and compassion, says: "They that be endued with so excellent a benefit of God, be called according to God's purpose in due season: they through grace obey the calling: they be justified freely: they be made sons of God by adoption: they be made like the image of his only begotten Son, Jesus Christ: they walk religiously in good works; and at length, by God's mercy, they attain to everlasting felicity."

Such a conception and display of the almighty wisdom, power, and love, is indeed "full of sweet, pleasant, and unspeakable comfort to godly persons, and such as feel in themselves the working of the Spirit of Christ mortifying the works of the flesh and their earthly members, and drawing up their minds to high and heavenly things: it doth greatly establish and confirm their faith of eternal salvation, to be enjoyed through Christ, and doth fervently kindle their love towards God."

Nearly allied to the consolation of a good hope through grace, as it respects our own personal state before God, is that of seeing its evidences shed lustre over the disposition and conduct of others. Bright was the exhibition of the union between true Christian enjoyment and Christian exertion, in the character whose moral and spiritual features I am attempting to delineate.

It seemed to be the first wish of her heart to prove to others, what God had already proved to her, that Jesus is "the way, and the truth, and the life." She desired to evince the reality of her calling, justification, and adoption into the family of God, by showing a conformity to the image of Christ, and by walking "religiously in good works:" she trusted that, in this path of faith and obedience, she should "at length, by God's mercy, attain to everlasting felicity."

I had the spiritual charge of another parish, adjoining to that in which I resided. It was a small district, and had but few inhabitants. The church was pleasantly situated on a rising bank, at the foot of a considerable hill. It was surrounded by trees, and had a rural, retired appearance. Close to the church-yard stood a large old mansion, which had formerly been the residence of an opulent and titled family; but it had long since been appropriated to the use of the estate as a farm-house. Its outward aspect bore considerable remains of ancient grandeur, and gave a pleasing character to the spot of ground on which the church stood.

In every direction the roads that led to this house of God possessed distinct but interesting features. One of them ascended between several rural cottages, from the sea-shore, which adjoined the lower part of the village street. Another winded round the curved sides of the adjacent hill, and was adorned, both above and below, with numerous sheep, feeding on the herbage of the down. A third road led to the church by a gently rising approach between high banks, covered with young trees, bushes, ivy, hedge-plants, and wild flowers.

From a point of land which commanded a view of all these several avenues, I used sometimes for a while to watch my congregation gradually assembling together at the hour of Sabbath worship. They were in some directions visible for a considerable distance. Gratifying associations of thought would form in my mind, as I contemplated their approach, and successive arrival, within the precincts of the house of prayer.

One day as I was thus occupied, during a short interval previous to the hour of divine service, I reflected on the joy which David experienced at the time he exclaimed: "I was glad when they said unto me, Let us go into the house of the Lord. Our feet shall stand within thy gates, O Jerusalem. Jerusalem is builded as a city that is compact together; whither the tribes go up, the tribes of the Lord, unto the testimony of Israel, to give thanks unto the name of the Lord."

I was led to reflect upon the various blessings connected with the establishment of public worship. "How many immortal souls are now gathering together to perform the all-important work of prayer and praise—to hear the word of God—to feed upon the bread of life! They are leaving their respective dwellings, and will soon be united together in the house of prayer. How beautifully does this represent the effect produced by the voice of the 'Good Shepherd,' calling his sheep from every part of the wilderness into his fold! As these fields, hills, and lanes, are now covered with men, women, and children, in various directions, drawing nearer to each other, and to the object of their journey's end; even so, 'many shall come from the east, and from the west, and from the north, and from the south, and shall sit down in the kingdom of God.'"

Who can rightly appreciate the value of such hours as these?—hours spent in learning the ways of holy pleasantness and the paths of heavenly peace— hours devoted to the service of God and of souls; in warning the sinner to flee from the wrath to come; in teaching the ignorant how to live and die; in preaching the gospel to the poor; in healing the broken- hearted; in declaring "deliverance to the captives, and recovering of sight to the blind."—"Blessed is the people that know the joyful sound: they shall walk, O Lord, in the light of thy countenance. In thy name they shall rejoice all the day, and in thy righteousness shall they be exalted."

My thoughts then pursued a train of reflection on the importance of the ministerial office, as connected in the purposes of God with the salvation of sinners. I inwardly prayed that those many individuals whom he had given me to instruct, might not, through my neglect or error, be as sheep having no shepherd, nor as the blind led by the blind; but rather that I might, in season and out of season, faithfully proclaim the simple and undisguised truths of the gospel, to the glory of God and the prosperity of his church.

At that instant, near the bottom of the enclosed lane which led to the church-yard, I observed a friend, whom, at such a distance from his home, I little expected to meet. It was the venerable Dairyman. He came up the ascent, leaning with one hand on his trusty staff, and with the other on the arm of a younger man, well known to me, who appeared to be much gratified in meeting with such a companion by the way.

My station was on the top of one of the banks which formed the hollow road beneath. They passed a few yards below me. I was concealed from their sight by a projecting tree. They were talking of the mercies of God, and the unsearchable riches of his grace. The Dairyman was telling his companion what a blessing the Lord had given him in his daughter. His countenance brightened as he named her, and called her his precious Betsy.

I met them at a stile not many yards beyond, and accompanied them to the church, which was hard by.

"Sir," said the old man, "I have brought a letter from my daughter, I hope I am in time for divine service. Seven miles has now become a long walk for me: I grow old and weak. I am very glad to see you, sir."

"How is your daughter?"

"Very poorly indeed, sir,—very poorly. The doctors say it is a decline. I sometimes hope she will get the better of it; but then again I have many fears. You know, sir, that I have cause to love and prize her. Oh, it would be such a trial! but the Lord knows what is best. Excuse my weakness, sir."

He put a letter into my hand, the perusal of which I reserved till afterwards, as the time was nigh for going into church.

The presence of this aged pilgrim, the peculiar reverence and affection with which he joined in the different parts of the service, excited many gratifying thoughts in my mind, such as rather furthered than interrupted devotion.

The train of reflection in which I had been engaged when I first discovered him on the road, at intervals recurred powerfully to my feelings, as I viewed that very congregation assembled together in the house of God, whose steps, in their approach towards it, I had watched with prayerful emotions.

"Here the rich and poor meet together in mutual acknowledgment that the Lord is the maker of them all; and that all are alike dependent creatures, looking up to one common Father to supply their wants, both temporal and spiritual.

"Again, likewise, will they meet together in the grave, that undistinguished receptacle of the opulent and the needy.

"And once more, at the judgment-seat of Christ shall the rich and the poor meet together, that 'every one may receive the things done in his body, according to that he hath done, whether it be good or bad.'

"How closely connected in the history of man are these three periods of a general meeting together?

"The house of prayer—the house appointed for all living—and the house not made with hands, eternal in the heavens. May we never separate these ideas from each other, but retain them in a sacred and profitable union! So shall our worshipping assemblies on earth be representative of the general assembly and church of the first-born, which are written in heaven."

When the congregation dispersed, I entered into discourse with the Dairyman and a few of the poor of my flock, whose minds were of the like disposition to his own. He seldom could speak long together without some reference to his dear child. He loved to tell how merciful his God had been to him, in the dutiful and affectionate attentions of his daughter. All real Christians feel a tender spiritual attachment towards those who have been the instrument of bringing them to an effectual knowledge of the way of salvation; but when that instrument is one so nearly allied, how dear does the relationship become!

If my friend the Dairyman was in any danger of falling into idolatry, his child would have been the idol of his affections. She was the prop and stay of her parents' declining years, and they scarcely knew how sufficiently to testify the gratitude of their hearts for the comfort and blessing which she was the means of affording them.

While he was relating several particulars of his family history to the others, I opened and read the following letter:—

"SIR,

"Once more I take the liberty to trouble you with a few lines. I received your letter with great pleasure, and thank you for it. I am now so weak that I am unable to walk to any public place of divine worship,—a privilege which has heretofore always so much strengthened and refreshed me. I used to go in anxious expectation to meet my God, and hold sweet communion with him; and I was seldom disappointed. In the means of grace all the channels of divine mercy are open to every heart that is lifted up to receive out of that divine fulness grace for grace. These are the times of refreshing from the presence of the Lord. How have I rejoiced to hear a faithful and lively messenger, just come, as it were, from communion with God at the throne of grace, with his heart warmed and filled with divine love, to speak to fallen sinners! Such a one has seemed to me as if his face shone as that of Moses did with the glory of God, when he came down from the mount, where he had been within the veil. May you, sir, imitate him, as he did Christ, that all may see and know that the Lord dwelleth with you, and that you dwell in him through the unity of the blessed Spirit. I trust you are no stranger to his divine teaching, aid, and assistance, in all you set your hand to do for the glory of God.

"I hope, sir, the sincerity of my wishes for your spiritual welfare will plead an excuse for the freedom of my address to you. I pray the

Giver of every perfect gift, that you may experience the mighty workings of his gracious Spirit in your heart and your ministry, and rest your all on the justifying and purifying blood of an expired Redeemer. Then will you triumph in his strength, and be enabled to say with the poet,—

'Shall I, through fear of feeble man,
The Spirit's course strive to restrain;
Or, undismayed in deed and word,
Be a true witness for my Lord?

Awed by a mortal's frown shall I
Conceal the word of God most high?
How then before thee shall I dare
To stand, or how thine anger bear?

Shall I, to soothe the unholy throng,
Soften thy truths and smooth my tongue,
To gain earth's gilded toys, or flee
The cross endured, my God, by thee?

What then is he whose scorn I dread.
Whose wrath or hate makes me afraid?
A man? an heir of death? a slave
To sin? a bubble on the wave?

Yea, let men rage, since thou wilt spread
Thy shadowing wings around my head:
Since in all pain thy tender love
Will still my sure refreshment prove.

Still shall the love of Christ restrain
To seek the wand'ring souls of men,
With cries, entreaties, tears to save,
And snatch them from the yawning grave.

For this let men revile my name,—
No cross I shun, I fear no shame:
All hail reproach, and welcome pain;
Only thy terrors, Lord, restrain.'

"I trust, sir, that you see what a glorious high calling yours is, and that you are one of those who walk humbly with God, that you may be taught of him in all things. Persons in your place are messengers of the most high God. Is it too much to say, they should live like the angels in all holiness, and be filled with love and zeal for men's souls? They are ambassadors, in Christ's stead, to persuade sinners to be reconciled to God. So that your calling is above that of angels: for they are *afterwards* to minister to the heirs of salvation; but the sinner must be *first* reconciled to God. And you are called on from day to day to intercede with man as his friend, that you may win souls to Christ. Christ is ascended up on high, to intercede with his Father for guilty sinners, and to plead for them the merits of his death. So that Christ and his faithful ministers, through the operation of the blessed Spirit, are co-workers together. Yet without him we can do nothing: our strength is his strength, and his is all the glory from first to last.

"It is my heart's prayer and desire, sir, that you may, by a living faith, cleave close to that blessed, exalted Lamb of God, who died to redeem us from sin—that you may have a sweet communion with Father, Son, and Spirit—that you may sink deep in humble love, and rise high in the life of God. Thus will you have such discoveries of the beauties of Christ and his eternal glory as will fill your heart with true delight.

"If I am not deceived, I wish myself to enjoy his gracious favour, more than all the treasures which earth can afford. I would in comparison look upon them with holy disdain, and as not worth an anxious thought, that they may not have power on my heart to draw or attract it from God, who is worthy of my highest esteem, and of all my affections. It should be our endeavour to set him always before us, that in all things we may act as in his immediate presence; that we may be filled with that holy fear, so that we may not dare wilfully to sin against him. We should earnestly entreat the Lord to mortify the power and working of sin and unbelief within us, by making Christ appear more and more precious in our eyes, and more dear to our hearts.

"It fills my heart with thankful recollections, while I attempt in this weak manner to speak of God's love to man. When I reflect on my past sins and his past mercies, I am assured, that if I had all the gifts of wise men and angels, I could never sufficiently describe my own inward sense of his undeserved love towards me. We can better enjoy these glorious apprehensions in our hearts than explain them to others. But, oh, how unworthy of them are we all! Consciousness of my own corruptions keeps me often low; yet faith and desire will easily mount on high, beseeching God that he would, according to the apostle's prayer, fill me with all his communicable fulness, in the gifts and graces of his Spirit; that I may walk well-pleasing before him, in all holy conversation, perfecting holiness in his fear.

"If I err in boldness, sir, pray pardon me, and in your next letter confirm my hope that you will be my counsellor and guide.

"I can only recompense your kindness to me by my prayers, that your own intercourse with God may be abundantly blessed to you and yours. I consider the Saviour saying to you, as he did to Peter, 'Lovest thou me?' And may your heartfelt experience be compelled to reply, 'Thou knowest all things, and thou knowest that I love thee' supremely! May he have evident marks of it in all your outward actions of love and humanity in feeding his flock, and in the inward fervour and affection of all your consecrated powers: that you may be zealously engaged in pulling down the strongholds of sin and Satan, and building up his Church; sowing the seeds of righteousness, and praying God to give the increase: that you may not labour for him in vain, but may see the trees bud and blossom, and bring forth fruit abundantly, to the praise and glory of your heavenly Master. In order to give you encouragement, he says, whosoever 'converteth a sinner from the error of his way shall save a soul from death;' and that will increase the brightness of your crown in glory. This hath Christ merited for his faithful ministers.

"I hope, sir, you will receive grace to be sincere in reproving sin, wherever you see it. You will find divine assistance, and all fear and shame taken from you. Great peace will be given to you, and wisdom, strength, and courage, according to your work. You will be as Paul; having much learning, you can speak to men in all stations in life, by God's assistance. The fear of offending them will never prevent you, when you consider the glory of God; and man's immortal soul is of more value than his present favour and esteem. In particular, you are in an office wherein you can visit *all* the sick. Man's extremity is often God's opportunity. In this way you may prove an instrument in his hand to do his work. Although he *can* work without means, yet his usual way is by means; and I trust you are a chosen vessel unto him, to prove his name and declare his truth to all men.

"Visiting the sick is a strict command, and a duty for every Christian. None can tell what good may be done. I wish it was never neglected, as it too often is. Many think that if they attend in the church, the minister to preach, and the people to hear, their duty is done. But more is required than this. May the Lord stir up the gift that is in his people and ministers, that they may have compassion on their fellow-sinners,—that they may never think it too late, but remember that while there is life there is hope!" Once more I pray, sir, pardon and excuse all my errors in judgment, and the ignorance that this is penned in; and may God bless you in all things, and particularly your friendship to me and my parents. What a comfort is family religion! I do not doubt but this is your desire, as it is mine, to say,—

'I and my house will serve the Lord,
But first obedient to his word
    I must myself appear;
By actions, words, and tempers show
That I my heavenly Master know,
    And serve with heart sincere.

I must the fair example set;
From those that on my pleasure wait
    The stumbling-block remove;
Their duty by my life explain,
And still in all my works maintain
    The dignity of love.

Easy to be entreated, mild,
Quickly appeased and reconciled,
    A follower of my God:
A saint indeed I long to be,
And lead my faithful family
    In the celestial road.

Lord, if thou dost the wish infuse,
A vessel fitted for thy use
    Into thy hands receive:
Work in me both to will and do,
And show them how believers true
    And real Christians live.

With all sufficient grace supply,
And then I'll come to testify
    The wonders of thy name,
Which saves from sin, the world, and hell:
Its power may every sinner feel,
    And every tongue proclaim!

Cleansed by the blood of Christ from sin,
I seek my relatives to win,
    And preach their sins forgiven;

Children, and wife, and servants seize,
And through the paths of pleasantness
    Conduct them all to heaven.'

"Living so much in a solitary way, books are my companions; and poetry which speaks of the love of God and the mercies of Christ is very sweet to my mind. This must be my excuse for troubling you to read verses which others have written. I have intended, if my declining state of health permit, to go to — for a few days. I say this lest you should call in expectation of seeing me during any part of next week. But my dear father and mother, for whose precious souls I am very anxious, will reap the benefit of your visit at all events.

"From your humble and unworthy servant,
"E— W—."

Having read it, I said to the father of my highly valued correspondent,—
"I thank you for being the bearer of this letter. Your daughter is a kind friend and faithful counsellor to me, as well as to you. Tell her how highly I esteem her friendship, and that I feel truly obliged for the many excellent sentiments which she has here expressed. Give her my blessing, and assure her that the oftener she writes the more thankful I shall be."
The Dairyman's enlivened eye gleamed with pleasure as I spoke. The praise of his Elizabeth was a string which could not be touched without causing every nerve of his whole frame to vibrate.
His voice half faltered as he spoke in reply; the tear started in his eyes; his hand trembled as I pressed it; his heart was full; he could only say,—
"Sir, a poor old man thanks you for your kindness to him and his family. God bless you, sir; I hope we shall soon see you again."
Thus we parted for that day.

PART V.

It has not unfrequently been observed, that when it is the Lord's pleasure to remove any of his faithful followers out of this life at an early period of their course, they make rapid progress in the experience of divine truth. The fruits of the Spirit ripen fast as they advance to the close of mortal existence. In particular, they grow in humility, through a deeper sense of inward corruption and a clearer view of the perfect character of the Saviour. Disease and bodily weakness make the thoughts of eternity recur with frequency and power. The great question of their own personal salvation, the quality of their faith, the sincerity of their love, and the purity of their hope, are in continual exercise.

Unseen realities at such a time occupy a larger portion of thought than before. The state of existence beyond the grave, the invisible world, the unalterable character of the dead, the future judgment, the total separation from everything earthly, the dissolution of body and spirit, and their re-union at the solemn hour of resurrection—these are subjects for their meditation, which call for serious earnestness of soul. Whatever consolations from the Spirit of God they may have enjoyed heretofore, they become now doubly anxious to examine and prove themselves whether they be indeed in the faith. In doing this, they sometimes pass through hidden conflicts of a dark and distressing nature; from which, however, they come forth like gold tried in the furnace. Awhile they may sow in tears, but soon they reap in joy.

Their religious feelings have then, perhaps, less of ecstasy, but more of serenity.

As the ears of corn ripen for the harvest, they bow their heads nearer to the ground. So it is with believers: they then see more than ever of their own imperfection, and often express their sense of it in strong language; yet they repose with a growing confidence on the love of God through Christ Jesus. The nearer they advance to their eternal rest, the more humble they become, but not the less useful in their sphere. They feel anxiously desirous of improving every talent they possess to the glory of God, knowing that the time is short.

I thought I observed the truth of these remarks fulfilled in the progressive state of mind of the Dairyman's daughter.

Declining health seemed to indicate the will of God concerning her. But her character, conduct, and experience of the Divine favour, increased in brightness as the setting sun of her mortal life approached its horizon. The last letter which, with the exception of a very short note, I ever received from her, I shall now transcribe. It appeared to me to bear the marks of a still deeper acquaintance with the workings of her own heart, and a more entire reliance upon the free mercy of God.

The original, while I copy it, strongly revives the image of the deceased, and the many profitable conversations which I once enjoyed in her company, and that of her parents. It again endears to me the recollections of cottage piety, and helps me to anticipate the joys of that day when the spirits of the glorified saints shall be re-united to their bodies, and be for ever with the Lord.

The writer of this and the preceding letters herself little imagined, when they were penned, that they would ever be submitted to the public eye; that they now are so, results from a conviction that the friends of the pious poor will estimate them according to their value; and a hope that it may please God to honour these memorials of the dead, to the effectual edification of the living.

"REV. SIR,

"In consequence of your kind permission, I take the liberty to trouble you with another of my ill-written letters; and I trust you have too much of your blessed Master's lowly, meek, and humble mind, to be offended with a poor, simple, ignorant creature, whose intentions are pure and sincere in writing. My desire is, that I, a weak vessel of his grace, may glorify his name for his goodness towards me. May the Lord direct me by his counsel and wisdom! May he overshadow me with his presence, that I may sit beneath the banner of his love, and find the consolations of his blessed Spirit sweet and refreshing to my soul.

"When I feel that I am nothing, and God is all in all, then I can willingly fly to him, saying, 'Lord, help me; Lord, teach me; be unto me my prophet, priest, and king. Let me know the teaching of thy grace, and the disclosing of thy love.' What nearness of access might we have, if we lived more near to God! What sweet communion might we have with a God of love! He is the great I AM. How glorious a name! Angels with trembling awe prostrate themselves before him, and in humble love adore and worship him. One says—

'While the first archangel sings,
He hides his face behind his wings.'
Unworthy as I am, I have found it by experience that the more I see of the greatness and goodness of God, and the nearer union I hope I have had with him through the Spirit of his love, the more humble and self-abased I have been.

"But every day I may say, 'Lord, how little I love thee, how far I live from thee, how little am I like thee in humility!' It is, nevertheless, my heart's desire to love and serve him better. I find the way in which God does more particularly bless me, is when I attend on the public ordinances of religion. These are the channels through which he conveys the riches of his grace and precious love to my soul. These I have often found to be indeed the time of refreshing and strengthening from the presence of the Lord. Then I can see my hope of an interest in the covenant of his love, and praise him for his mercy to the greatest of sinners.

"I earnestly wish to be more established in his ways, and to honour him in the path of duty, whilst I enjoy the smiles of his favour. In the midst of all outward afflictions I pray that I may know Christ and the power of his resurrection within my soul. If I were always thus, my summer would last all the year; my will would then be sweetly lost in God's will, and I should feel a resignation in every dispensation of his providence and his grace, saying, 'Good is the will of the Lord: Infinite Wisdom cannot err.' Then would patience have its perfect work.

"But, alas! sin and unbelief often, too often, interrupt these frames, and lay me low before God in tears of sorrow. I often think what a happiness it would be if his love were so fixed in my heart that I might willingly obey him with alacrity and delight, and gradually mortify the power of self-will, passion, and pride. This can only arise from a good hope through grace that we are washed in that precious blood which cleanses us from every sinful stain, and makes us new creatures in Christ. Oh that we may be the happy witnesses of the saving power and virtue of that healing stream which flows from the fountain of everlasting love!

"Sir, my faith is often exceedingly weak: can you be so kind as to tell me what you have found to be the most effectual means of strengthening it? I often think how plainly the Lord declares, 'Believe only, and thou shalt be saved. Only have faith; all things are possible to him that has it.' How I wish that we could remove all those mountains that hinder and obstruct the light of his grace; so that, having full access unto God through that ever-blessed Spirit, we might lovingly commune with him as with the dearest of friends. What favour does God bestow on worms! And yet we love to murmur and complain. He may well say, 'What should I have done more, that I have not done? or wherein have I proved unfaithful or unkind to my faithless, backsliding children?'

"Sir, I pray that I may not grieve him, as I have done, any more. I want your counsel and your prayers for me in this matter. How refreshing is the sight of one that truly loves God, that bears his image and likeness!

"But delightful as is conversation with true believers on earth, whose hearts are lifted up to things above, yet what is this to that happy day which will admit us into more bright realms; where we shall for ever behold a God of love in the smiling face of his Son, who is the express image of his Father and the brightness of his glory! Then, if found in him, we shall be received by the innumerable host of angels who wait around his throne.

"In the meantime, sir, may I take up my cross, and manfully fight under Him who, for the glory that was set before him, endured the cross, despising the shame, and is now set down at his Father's right hand in majesty. I thank you for the kind liberty you have given me of writing to you. I feel my health declining, and I find a relief, during an hour of pain and weakness, in communicating these thoughts to you.

"I hope, sir, you go on your way rejoicing; that you are enabled to thank Him who is the giver of every good gift, spiritual, temporal, and providential, for blessings to yourself and your ministry. I do not doubt but you often meet with circumstances which are not pleasing to nature; yet, by the blessing of God, they will be all profitable in the end. They are kindly designed by grace to make and keep us humble. The difficulties which you spoke of to me some time since will, I trust, disappear.

"My dear father and mother are as well as usual in bodily health; and, I hope, grow in grace, and in the knowledge and love of Jesus Christ. My chief desire to live is for their sakes. It now seems long since we have seen you. I am almost ashamed to request you to come to our little cottage, to visit those who are so much below your station in life. But if you cannot come, we shall be very glad if you will write a few lines. I ought to make an excuse for my letter, I spell so badly: this was a great neglect when I was young. I gave myself greatly to reading, but not to the other, and now I am too weak and feeble to learn much.

"I hear sometimes of persons growing serious in your congregation: it gives me joy; and, if true, I am sure it does so to yourself. I long for the pure gospel of Christ to be preached in every church in the world, and for the time when all shall know, love, and fear the Lord; and the uniting Spirit of God shall make them of one heart and mind in Christ our great head. Your greatest joy, I know, will be in labouring much for the glory of God in the salvation of men's souls. You serve a good Master. You have a sure reward. I pray God to give you strength according to your day.

"Pray, sir, do not be offended at the freedom and manner of my writing. My parents' duty and love to you are sent with these lines from

"Your humble servant in Christ,
"E— W—."

Epistolary communications, when written in sincerity of heart, afford genuine portraits of the mind. May the foregoing be viewed with Christian candour, and consecrated to affectionate memory!

PART VI.

Travellers, as they pass through the country, usually stop to inquire whose are the splendid mansions which they discover among the woods and plains around them. The families, titles, fortune, or character of the respective owners, engage much attention. Perhaps their houses are exhibited to the admiring stranger. The elegant rooms, costly furniture, valuable paintings, beautiful gardens and shrubberies, are universally approved; while the rank, fashion, taste, and riches of the possessor, afford ample materials for entertaining discussion. In the meantime, the lowly cottage of the poor husbandman is passed by as scarcely deserving of notice. Yet, perchance, such a cottage may often contain a treasure of infinitely more value than the sumptuous palace of the rich man— even "the pearl of great price." If this be set in the heart of the poor cottager, it proves a gem of unspeakable worth, and will shine among the brightest ornaments of the Redeemer's crown, in that day when he maketh up his "jewels."

Hence the Christian traveller, while in common with others he bestows his due share of applause on the decorations of the rich, and is not insensible to the beauties and magnificence which are the lawfully allowed appendages of rank and fortune, cannot overlook the humbler dwelling of the poor. And if he should find that true piety and grace beneath the thatched roof which he has in vain looked for amidst the worldly grandeur of the rich, he remembers the declarations in the word of God. He sees with admiration that the high and lofty One, that inhabiteth eternity, whose name is Holy, who dwelleth in the high and holy place, dwelleth with *him also* that is of a contrite and humble spirit (Isa. lvii. 15); and although heaven is his throne, and the earth his footstool, yet, when a house is to be built and a place of rest to be sought for himself, he says, "To this man will I look, even to him that is poor and of a contrite spirit, and trembleth at my word" (Isa. lxvi. 2).

When a house is thus tenanted, Faith beholds this inscription written on the walls, *The Lord lives here.* Faith, therefore, cannot pass it by unnoticed, but loves to lift up the latch of the door, and to sit down and converse with the poor, although perhaps despised, inhabitant. Many a sweet interview does Faith obtain, when she thus takes her walks abroad. Many such a sweet interview have I myself enjoyed beneath the roof where dwelt the Dairyman and his little family.

I soon perceived that his daughter's health was rapidly on the decline. The pale, wasting consumption, which is the Lord's instrument for removing so many thousands every year from the land of the living made hasty strides on her constitution. The hollow eye, the distressing cough, and the often too flattering flush on the cheek, foretold the approach of death.

What a field for usefulness and affectionate attention, on the part of ministers and Christian friends, is opened by the frequent attacks and lingering process of *consumptive* illness! How many such precious opportunities are daily lost, where Providence seems in so marked a way to afford time and space for serious and godly instruction! Of how many may it be said, "The way of peace have they not known!" for not one friend ever came nigh, to warn them to "flee from the wrath to come."

But the Dairyman's daughter was happily made acquainted with the things which belonged to her everlasting peace, before the present disease had taken root in her constitution. In my visits to her, I went rather to receive information than to impart it. Her mind was abundantly stored with divine truths, and her conversation was truly edifying. The recollection of it will ever produce a thankful sensation in my heart.

I one day received a short note to the following effect:—
"DEAR SIR,

"I should be very glad, if your convenience will allow, that you will come and see a poor unworthy sinner. My hour-glass is nearly run out, but I hope I can see Christ to be precious to my soul. Your conversation has often been blessed to me, and I now feel the need of it more than ever. My father and mother send their duty to you. From

"Your obedient and unworthy servant,
"E— W—."

I obeyed the summons that same afternoon. On my arrival at the Dairyman's cottage, his wife opened the door. The tears streamed down her cheek, as she silently shook her head. Her heart was full. She tried to speak, but could not. I took her by the hand, and said—

"My good friend, all is right, and as the Lord of wisdom and mercy directs."

"Oh, my Betsy, my dear girl, is so bad, sir. What shall I do without her? I thought I should have gone first to the grave; but—"

"But the Lord sees good that, before you die yourself you should behold your child safe home to glory. Is there no mercy in this?"

"Oh, dear sir! I am very old and very weak; and she is a dear child, the staff and prop of a poor old creature as I am."

As I advanced, I saw Elizabeth sitting by the fireside, supported in an arm-chair by pillows, with every mark of rapid decline and approaching death. A sweet smile of friendly complacency enlightened her pale countenance, as she said—

"This is very kind indeed, sir, to come so soon after I sent to you. You find me daily wasting away, and I cannot have long to continue here. My flesh and my heart fail; but God is the strength of my weak heart, and I trust will be my portion for ever."

The conversation was occasionally interrupted by her cough and want of breath. Her tone of voice was clear, though feeble; her manner solemn and collected; and her eye, though more dim than formerly, by no means wanting in liveliness as she spoke. I had frequently admired the superior language in which she expressed her ideas, as well as the scriptural consistency with which she communicated her thoughts. She had a good natural understanding, and grace, as is generally the case, had much improved it. On the present occasion I could not help thinking she was peculiarly favoured. The whole strength of gracious and natural attainments seemed to be in full exercise.

After taking my seat between the daughter and the mother (the latter fixing her fond eyes upon her child with great anxiety while we were conversing), I said to Elizabeth—

"I hope you enjoy a sense of the divine presence, and can rest all upon Him who has 'been with thee,' and has 'kept thee in all places where thou hast gone,' and will bring thee into 'the land of pure delight, where saints immortal reign.'"

"Sir, I think I can. My mind has lately been sometimes clouded, but I believe it has been partly owing to the great weakness and suffering of my bodily frame, and partly to the envy of my spiritual enemy, who wants to persuade me that Christ has no love for me, and that I have been a self-deceiver."

"And do you give way to his suggestions? Can you doubt, amidst such numerous tokens of past and present mercy?"

"No, sir, I mostly am enabled to preserve a clear evidence of his love. I do not wish to add to my other sins that of denying his manifest goodness to my soul—I would acknowledge it to his praise and glory."

"What is your present view of the state in which you were before you felt seriously concerned about the salvation of your soul?"

"Sir, I was a proud, thoughtless girl; fond of dress and finery. I loved the world, and the things that are in the world. I lived in service among worldly people, and never had the happiness of being in a family where worship was regarded, and the souls of the servants cared for, either by master or mistress. I went once on a Sunday to church, more to see and be seen than to pray or hear the word of God. I thought I was quite good enough to be saved, and disliked, and often laughed at, religious people. I was in great darkness; I knew nothing of the way of salvation. I never prayed, nor was sensible of the awful danger of a prayerless state. I wished to maintain the character of a good servant, and was much lifted up whenever I met with applause. I was tolerably moral and decent in my conduct, from motives of carnal and worldly policy; but I was a stranger to God and Christ. I neglected my soul; and had I died in such a state, hell must, and would justly, have been my portion."

"How long is it since you heard the sermon which, you hope, through God's blessing, effected your conversion?"

"About five years ago."

"How was it brought about?"

"It was reported that a Mr. —, who was detained by contrary winds from embarking on board ship as chaplain to a distant part of the world, was to preach at church. Many advised me not to go, for fear he should turn my head, as they said he held strange notions. But curiosity, and an opportunity of appearing in a new gown, which I was very proud of, induced me to ask leave of my mistress to go. Indeed, sir, I had no better motives than vanity and curiosity. Yet thus it pleased the Lord to order it for his own glory.

"I accordingly went to church, and saw a great crowd of people collected together. I often think of the contrary states of my mind during the former and latter part of the service. For a while, regardless of the worship of God, I looked around me, and was anxious to attract notice myself. My dress, like that of too many gay, vain, and silly servant girls, was much above my station, and very different from that which becomes an humble sinner, who has a modest sense of propriety and decency. The state of my mind was visible enough from the foolish finery of my apparel.

"At length the clergyman gave out his text: 'Be ye clothed with humility.' He drew a comparison between the clothing of the body with that of the soul. At a very early part of his discourse I began to feel ashamed of my passion for fine dressing and apparel; but when he came to describe the garment of salvation with which a Christian is clothed, I felt a powerful discovery of the nakedness of my own soul. I saw that I had neither the humility mentioned in the text, nor any one part of the true Christian character. I looked at my gay dress, and blushed for shame on account of my pride. I looked at the minister, and he seemed to me as a messenger sent from heaven to open my eyes. I looked at the congregation, and wondered whether any one else felt as I did. I looked at my heart, and it appeared full of iniquity. I trembled as he spoke, and yet I felt a great drawing of heart to the words he uttered.

"He opened the riches of divine grace in God's method of saving the sinner. I was astonished at what I had been doing all the days of my life. He described the meek, lowly, and humble example of Christ; I felt proud, lofty, vain, and self-consequential. He represented Christ as 'Wisdom;' I felt my ignorance. He held him forth as 'Righteousness;' I was convinced of my own guilt. He proved him to be 'Sanctification;' I saw my corruption. He proclaimed him as 'Redemption;' I felt my slavery to sin and my captivity to Satan. He concluded with an animated address to sinners, in which he exhorted them to flee from the wrath to come, to cast off the love of outward ornament, to put on Jesus Christ, and be clothed with true humility.

"From that hour I never lost sight of the value of my soul and the danger of a sinful state. I inwardly blessed God for the sermon, although my mind was in a state of great confusion.

"The preacher had brought forward the ruling passion of my heart, which was pride in outward dress; and by the grace of God it was made instrumental to the awakening of my soul. Happy, sir, would it be if many a poor girl, like myself, were turned from the love of outward adorning and putting on of fine apparel, to seek that which is not corruptible, even the ornament of a meek and quiet spirit, which is in the sight of God of great price.

"The greatest part of the congregation, unused to such faithful and scriptural sermons, disliked and complained of the severity of the preacher; while a few, as I afterwards found, like myself, were deeply affected, and earnestly wished to hear him again. But he preached there no more.

"From that time I was led, through a course of private prayer, reading, and meditation, to see my lost state as a sinner, and the great mercy of God through

Jesus Christ, in raising sinful dust and ashes to a share in the glorious happiness of heaven. And, O sir! what a Saviour I have found! He is more than I could ask or desire. In his fulness I have found all that my poverty could need; in his bosom I have found a resting- place from all sin and sorrow; in his word I have found strength against doubt and unbelief."

"Were you not soon convinced," I said, "that your salvation must be an act of entire grace on the part of God, wholly independent of your own previous works or deservings?"

"Dear sir, what were my works, before I heard that sermon, but evil, carnal, selfish, and ungodly! The thoughts of my heart, from my youth upward, were only evil, and that continually. And my deservings, what were they, but the deservings of a fallen, depraved, careless soul, that regarded neither law nor gospel! Yes, sir, I immediately saw that if ever I were saved, it must be by the free mercy of God, and that the whole praise and honour of the work would be his from first to last."

"What change did you perceive in yourself with respect to the world?"

"It appeared all vanity and vexation of spirit. I found it necessary to my peace of mind to come out from among them, and be separate. I gave myself to prayer; and many a happy hour of secret delight I enjoyed in communion with God. Often I mourned over my sins, and sometimes had a great conflict, through unbelief, fear, temptation to return back again to my old ways, and a variety of difficulties which lay in my way. But He who loved me with an everlasting love drew me by his loving-kindness, showed me the way of peace, gradually strengthened me in my resolutions of leading a new life, and taught me, that while without him I could do nothing, I yet might do all things through his strength."

"Did you not find many difficulties in your situation, owing to your change of principle and practice?"

"Yes, sir, every day of my life. I was laughed at by some, scolded at by others, scorned by enemies, and pitied by friends. I was called hypocrite, saint, false deceiver, and many more names, which were meant to render me hateful in the sight of the world. But I esteemed the reproach of the cross an honour. I forgave and prayed for my persecutors, and remembered how very lately I had acted the same part towards others myself. I thought also that Christ endured the contradiction of sinners; and, as the disciple is not above his Master, I was glad to be in any way conformed to his sufferings."

"Did you not then feel for your family at home?"

"Yes, that I did indeed, sir; they were never out of my thoughts. I prayed continually for them, and had a longing desire to do them good. In particular, I felt for my father and mother, as they were getting into years, and were very ignorant and dark in matters of religion."

"Ay," interrupted her mother, sobbing, "ignorant and dark, sinful and miserable we were, till this dear Betsy—this dear Betsy—this dear child, sir— brought Christ Jesus home to her poor father and mother's house."

"No, dearest mother, say rather, Christ Jesus brought your poor daughter home to tell you what he had done for her soul, and I hope, to do the same for yours."

At that moment the Dairyman came in with two pails of milk hanging from the yoke on his shoulders. He had stood behind the half-opened door for a few minutes, and heard the last sentences spoken by his wife and daughter.

"Blessing and mercy upon her!" said he, "it is very true; she left a good place of service on purpose to live with us, that she might help us both in soul and body. Sir, don't she look very ill? I think, sir, we sha'n't have her here long."

"Leave that to the Lord," said Elizabeth. "All our times are in his hand, and happy it is that they are. I am willing to go; are you not willing, my father, to part with me into *his* hands, who gave me to you at first?"

"Ask me any question in the world but that," said the weeping father.

"I know," said she, "you wish me to be happy."

"I do, I do," answered he; "let the Lord do with you and us as best pleases him."

I then asked her on what her present consolations chiefly depended, in the prospect of approaching death.

"Entirely, sir, on my view of Christ. When I look at myself, many sins, infirmities, and imperfections cloud the image of Christ which I want to see in my own heart. But when I look at the Saviour himself, he is altogether lovely; there is not one spot in his countenance, nor one cloud over all his perfections.

"I think of his coming in the flesh, and it reconciles me to the sufferings of the body; for he had them as well as I. I think of his temptations, and believe that he is able to succour me when I am tempted. Then I think of his cross, and learn to bear my own. I reflect on his death, and long to die unto sin, so that it may no longer have dominion over me. I sometimes think on his resurrection, and trust that he has given me a part in it, for I feel that my affections are set upon things above. Chiefly I take comfort in thinking of him as at the right hand of the Father, pleading my cause, and rendering acceptable even my feeble prayers, both for myself, and, as I hope, for my dear friends.

"These are the views which, through mercy, I have of my Saviour's goodness; and they have made me wish and strive in my poor way to serve him, to give myself up to him, and to labour to do my duty in that state of life into which it has pleased God to call me.

"A thousand times I should have fallen and fainted, if he had not upheld me. I feel that I am nothing without him. He is all in all.

"Just so far as I can cast my care upon him, I find strength to do his will. May he give me grace to trust him till the last moment! I do not fear death, because I believe that he has taken away its sting. And oh! what happiness beyond! Tell me, sir, whether you think I am right. I hope I am under no delusion. I dare not look for my hope in anything short of the entire fulness of Christ. When I ask my own heart a question, I am afraid to trust it, for it is treacherous, and has often deceived me; but when I ask Christ, he answers me with promises that strengthen and refresh me, and leave me no room to doubt his power and will to save. I am in his hands, and would remain there; and I do believe that he will never leave nor forsake me, but will perfect the thing that concerns me. He loved me and gave himself for me, and I believe that his gifts and callings are without repentance. In this hope I live, in this hope I wish to die."

I looked around me, as she was speaking, and thought, "Surely this is none other than the house of God, and the gate of heaven." Everything appeared neat, cleanly, and interesting. The afternoon had been rather overcast with dark clouds; but just now the setting sun shone brightly and somewhat suddenly into the room. It was reflected from three or four rows of bright pewter plates and white earthenware, arranged on shelves against the wall: it also gave brilliancy to a few prints of sacred subjects that hung there also, and served for monitors of the birth, baptism, crucifixion, and resurrection of Christ.

A large map of Jerusalem, and a hieroglyphic of "the old and new man," completed the decorations on that side of the room. Clean as was the whitewashed wall, it was not cleaner than the rest of the place and its furniture. Seldom had the sun enlightened a house where order and general neatness (those sure attendants of pious poverty) were more conspicuous.

This gleam of setting sunshine was emblematical of the bright and serene close of this young Christian's departing season. One ray happened to be reflected from a little looking-glass upon her face. Amidst her pallid and decaying features there appeared a calm resignation, triumphant confidence, unaffected humility, and tender anxiety, which fully declared the feelings of her heart.

Some further affectionate conversation and a short prayer closed this interview.

As I rode home by departing daylight, a solemn tranquillity reigned throughout the scene. The gentle lowing of cattle, the bleating of sheep just penned in their folds, the humming of the insects of the night, the distant murmurs of the sea, the last notes of the birds of day, and the first warblings of the nightingale, broke upon the ear, and served rather to increase than lessen the peaceful serenity of the evening, and its corresponding effects on my own mind. It invited and cherished just such meditations as my visit had already inspired. Natural scenery, when viewed in a Christian mirror, frequently affords very beautiful illustrations of divine truths. We are highly favoured when we can enjoy them, and at the same time draw near to God in them.

PART VII.

It is a pleasing consideration, that amidst the spiritual darkness which unhappily prevails in many parts of the land, God nevertheless has a people. It not unfrequently happens that single individuals are to be found, who, though very disadvantageously situated with regard to the ordinary means of grace, have received truly saving impressions, and, through a blessing on secret meditation, reading, and prayer, are led to the closest communion with God, and become eminently devoted Christians. It is the no small error of too many professors of the present day, to overlook or undervalue the instances of this kind which exist. The religious profession and opinions of some have too much of mere *machinery* in their composition. If every wheel, pivot, chain, spring, cog, or pinion, be not exactly in its place, or move not precisely according to a favourite and prescribed system, the whole is rejected as unworthy of regard. But happily "the Lord knoweth them that are his;" nor is the impression of his own seal wanting to characterize some who, in comparative seclusion from the religious world, "name the name of Christ and depart from iniquity."

There are some real Christians so peculiarly circumstanced in this respect as to illustrate the poet's comparison,—

"Full many a gem of purest ray serene
    The dark unfathomed caves of ocean bear;
Full many a flower is born to blush unseen,
    And waste its sweetness on the desert air."

Yet this was not altogether the case with the Dairyman's daughter. Her religion had indeed ripened in seclusion from the world, and she was intimately known but to few; but she lived usefully, departed most happily, and left a shining track behind her. While I attempt a faint delineation of it, may I catch its influence, and become, through inexpressible mercy, a follower of "them who through faith and patience inherit the promises!"

From the time wherein I visited her, as described in my last paper, I considered her end as fast approaching. One day I received a hasty summons to inform me that she was dying. It was brought by a soldier, whose countenance bespoke seriousness, good sense, and piety.

"I am sent, sir, by the father and mother of Elizabeth W—, at her own particular request, to say how much they all wish to see you. She is going *home*, sir, very fast indeed."

"Have you known her long?"

"About a month, sir. I love to visit the sick, and hearing of her case from a person who lives close by our camp, I went to see her. I bless God that ever I did go. Her conversation has been very profitable to me."

"I rejoice," said I, "to see in you, as I trust, a *brother soldier*. Though we differ in our outward regimentals, I hope we serve under the same spiritual Captain. I will go with you."

My horse was soon ready. My military companion walked by my side, and gratified me with very sensible and pious conversation. He related some remarkable testimonies of the excellent disposition of the Dairyman's daughter, as they appeared from recent intercourse which he had had with her.

"She is a bright diamond, sir," said the soldier, "and will soon shine brighter than any diamond upon earth."

We passed through lanes and fields, over hills and valleys, by open and retired paths, sometimes crossing over and sometimes following the windings of a little brook which gently murmured by the road side. Conversation beguiled the distance, and shortened the apparent time of our journey, till we were nearly arrived at the Dairyman's cottage.

As we approached it, we became silent. Thoughts of death, eternity, and salvation, inspired by the sight of a house where a dying believer lay, filled my own mind, and, I doubt not, that of my companion also.

No living object yet appeared, except the Dairyman's dog, keeping a kind of mute watch at the door; for he did not, as formerly, bark at my approach. He seemed to partake so far of the feelings appropriate to the circumstances of the family, as not to wish to give a hasty or painful alarm. He came forward to the little wicket-gate, then looked back at the house door, as if conscious there was sorrow within. It was as if he wanted to say, "Tread softly over the threshold, as you enter the house of mourning; for my master's heart is full of grief."

The soldier took my horse and tied it up in a shed. A solemn serenity appeared to surround the whole place; it was only interrupted by the breezes passing through the large elm-trees which stood near the house, and which my imagination indulged itself in thinking were plaintive sighs of sorrow. I gently opened the door. No one appeared, and all was still silent. The soldier followed. We came to the foot of the stairs.

"They are come!" said a voice, which I knew to be the father's; "they are come!"

He appeared at the top. I gave him my hand, and said nothing. On entering the room above, I saw the aged mother and her son supporting the much-loved daughter and sister: the son's wife sat weeping in a window- seat, with a child on her lap: two or three persons attended in the room to discharge any office which friendship or necessity might require.

I sat down by the bedside. The mother could not weep, but now and then sighed deeply, as she alternately looked at Elizabeth and at me. The big tear rolled down the brother's cheek, and testified an affectionate regard. The good old man stood at the foot of the bed, leaning upon the post, and unable to take his eyes off the child from whom he was so soon to part.

Elizabeth's eyes were closed, and as yet she perceived me not. But over her face, though pale, sunk, and hollow, the peace of God, which passeth all understanding, had cast a triumphant calm.

The soldier, after a short pause, silently reached out his Bible towards me, pointing with his finger at 1 Cor. xv. 55, 56, 57. I then broke silence by reading the passage, "O death, where is thy sting? O grave, where is thy victory? The sting of death is sin; and the strength of sin is the law. But thanks be to God, which giveth us the victory through our Lord Jesus Christ."

At the sound of these words her eyes opened, and something like a ray of divine light beamed on her countenance as she said, "Victory! victory! through our Lord Jesus Christ."

She relapsed again, taking no further notice of any one present.

"God be praised for the triumph of faith!" said I.

"Amen!" replied the soldier.

The Dairyman's uplifted eye showed that the Amen was in his heart, though his tongue failed to utter it.

A short struggling for breath took place in the dying young woman, which was soon over; and then I said to her,—

"My dear friend, do you not feel that you are supported?"

"The Lord deals very gently with me," she replied.

"Are not his promises now very precious to you?"

"They are all yea and amen in Christ Jesus."

"Are you in much bodily pain?"

"So little that I almost forget it."

"How good the Lord is!"

"And how unworthy am I!"

"You are going to see him as he is."

"I think—I hope—I believe that I am."

She again fell into a short slumber.

Looking at her mother, I said, "What a mercy to have a child so near heaven as yours is!"

"And what a mercy," she replied, in broken accents, "if her poor old mother might but follow her there! But, sir, it is so hard to part!"

"I hope through grace by faith you will soon meet to part no more; it will be but a little while."

"Sir," said the Dairyman, "that thought supports me, and the Lord's goodness makes me feel more reconciled than I was."

"Father—mother," said the reviving daughter, "He is good to me—trust Him, praise Him evermore."

"Sir," added she, in a faint voice, "I want to thank you for your kindness to me—I want to ask a favour;—you buried my sister—will you do the same for me?"

"All shall be as you wish, if God permit," I replied.

"Thank you, sir, thank you—I have another favour to ask—When I am gone, remember my father and mother. They are old, but I hope the good work is begun in their souls—My prayers are heard—Pray come and see them—I cannot speak much, but I want to speak for their sakes—Sir, remember them."

The aged parents now sighed and sobbed aloud, uttering broken sentences, and gained some relief by such an expression of their feelings.

At length I said to Elizabeth, "Do you experience any doubts or temptations on the subject of your eternal safety?"

"No, sir. The Lord deals very gently with me, and gives me peace."

"What are your views of the dark valley of death, now that you are passing through it?"

"It is *not* dark."

"Why so?"

"My Lord is *there*, and he is my light and my salvation."

"Have you any fears of more bodily suffering?"

"The Lord deals so gently with me, I can trust him."

Something of a convulsion came on. When it was past she said again and again,—

"The Lord deals very gently with me. Lord, I am thine; save me—Blessed Jesus—precious Saviour—His blood cleanseth from all sin—Who shall separate?—His name is Wonderful—Thanks be to God—He giveth the victory—I, even I, am saved—O grace, mercy, and wonder!—Lord, receive my spirit!—Dear sir—dear father, mother, friends, I am going—but all is well, well, well—."

She relapsed again. We knelt down to prayer. The Lord was in the midst of us, and blessed us.

She did not again revive while I remained, nor ever speak any more words which could be understood. She slumbered for about ten hours, and at last sweetly fell asleep in the arms of that Lord who had dealt so gently with her.

I left the house an hour after she had ceased to speak. I pressed her hand as I was taking leave, and said, "Christ is the resurrection and the life." She gently returned the pressure, but could neither open her eyes nor utter a reply.

I never had witnessed a scene so impressive as this before. It completely filled my imagination as I returned home.

"Farewell," thought I, "dear friend, till the morning of an eternal day shall renew our personal intercourse. Thou wast a brand plucked from the burning, that thou mightest become a star shining in the firmament of glory. I have seen thy light and thy good works, and will therefore glorify our Father which is in heaven. I have seen, in thy example, what it is to be a sinner freely saved by grace. I have learned from thee, as in a living mirror, *who* it is that begins, continues, and ends the work of faith and love. Jesus is all in all: he will and shall be glorified. He won the crown, and alone deserves to wear it. May no one attempt to rob him of his glory! He saves, and saves to the uttermost. Farewell dear sister in the Lord. Thy flesh and thy heart may fail; but God is the strength of thy heart, and shall be thy portion for ever."

PART VIII.

Who can conceive or estimate the nature of that change which the soul of a believer must experience at the moment when, quitting its tabernacle of clay, it suddenly enters into the presence of God? If, even while "we see through a glass darkly," the views of divine love and wisdom are so delightful to the eye of faith; what must be the glorious vision of God, when seen face to face! If it be so valued a privilege here on earth to enjoy the communion of saints, and to take sweet counsel together with our fellow-travellers towards the heavenly kingdom; what shall we see and know when we finally "come unto mount Sion, and unto the city of the living God, the heavenly Jerusalem, and to an innumerable company of angels, to the general assembly and church of the first-born, which are written in heaven, and to God the Judge of all, and to the spirits of just men made perfect, and to Jesus the mediator of the new covenant?"

If, during the sighs and tears of a mortal pilgrimage, the consolations of the Spirit are so precious and the hope full of immortality is so animating to the soul; what heart can conceive, or what tongue utter its superior joys, when arrived at that state where sighing and sorrow flee away, and the tears shall be wiped from every eye?

Such ideas were powerfully associated together in my imagination, as I travelled onward to the house where, in solemn preparation for the grave, lay the remains of the Dairyman's daughter.

She had breathed her last shortly after the visit related in my former account. Permission was obtained, as before in the case of her sister, that I should perform the funeral service. Many pleasing yet melancholy thoughts were connected with the fulfilment of this task. I retraced the numerous and important conversations which I had held with her. But these could now no longer be maintained on earth. I reflected on the interesting and improving nature of *Christian* friendships, whether formed in palaces or in cottages; and felt thankful that I had so long enjoyed that privilege with the subject of this memorial. I then indulged a selfish sigh for a moment, on thinking that I could no longer hear the great truths of Christianity uttered by one who had drunk so deep of the waters of the river of life. But the rising murmur was checked by the animating thought, "She is gone to eternal rest—could I wish her back again in this vale of tears?"

At that moment the first sound of a tolling bell struck my ear. It proceeded from a village church in the valley directly beneath the ridge of a high hill, over which I had taken my way. It was Elizabeth's funeral knell.

The sound was solemn; and, in ascending to the elevated spot over which I rode, it acquired a peculiar tone and character. Tolling at slow and regular intervals, (as was customary for a considerable time previous to the hour of burial,) the bell, as it were, proclaimed the blessedness of the dead who die in the Lord, and also the necessity of the living pondering these things, and laying them to heart. It seemed to say, "Hear my warning voice, thou son of man.

There is but a step between thee and death. Arise, prepare thine house; for thou shalt die, and not live."

The scenery was in unison with that tranquil frame of mind which is most suitable for holy meditation. A rich and fruitful valley lay immediately beneath; it was adorned with corn fields and pastures, through which a small river winded in a variety of directions, and many herds grazed upon its banks. A fine range of opposite hills, covered with grazing flocks, terminated with a bold sweep into the ocean, whose blue waves appeared at a distance beyond. Several villages, hamlets, and churches, were scattered in the valley. The noble mansions of the rich, and the lowly cottages of the poor, added their respective features to the landscape. The air was mild, and the declining sun occasioned a beautiful interchange of light and shade upon the sides of the hills. In the midst of this scene, the chief sound that arrested attention was the bell tolling for the funeral of the Dairyman's daughter.

Do any of my readers inquire why I describe so minutely the circumstances of prospect and scenery which may be connected with the incidents I relate? My reply is, that the God of redemption is the God of creation likewise; and that we are taught in every part of the word of God to unite the admiration of the beauties and wonders of nature to every other motive for devotion. When David considered the heavens, the work of God's fingers, the moon and the stars which he has ordained, he was thereby led to the deepest humiliation of heart before his Maker. And when he viewed the sheep and the oxen and the beasts of the field, the fowls of the air and the fish of the sea, he was constrained to cry out, "O Lord, our Lord, how excellent is thy name in all the earth!"

I am the poor man's friend, and wish more especially that every poor labouring man should know how to connect the goodness of God in creation and providence with the unsearchable riches of his grace in the salvation of a sinner. And where can he learn this lesson more instructively than in looking around the fields where his labour is appointed, and there tracing the handiwork of God in all that he beholds? Such meditations have often afforded me both profit and pleasure, and I wish my readers to share them with me.

The Dairyman's cottage was rather more than a mile distant from the church. A lane, quite overshadowed with trees and high hedges, led from the foot of the hill to his dwelling. It was impossible at that time to overlook the suitable gloom of such an approach to the house of mourning.

I found, on my entrance, that several Christian friends, from different parts of the neighbourhood, had assembled together, to pay their last tribute of esteem and regard to the memory of the Dairyman's daughter. Several of them had first become acquainted with her during the latter stage of her illness; some few had maintained an affectionate intercourse with her for a longer period; but all seemed anxious to manifest their respect for one who was endeared to them by such striking testimonies of true Christianity.

I was requested to go into the chamber where the relatives and a few other friends were gone to take a last look at the remains of Elizabeth.

It is not easy to describe the sensation which the mind experiences on the first sight of a dead countenance, which, when living, was loved and esteemed for the sake of that soul which used to give it animation. A deep and awful view of the separation that has taken place between the soul and body of the deceased, since we last beheld them, occupies the feelings: our friend seems to be both near, and yet far off. The most interesting and valuable part is fled away; what remains is but the earthly, perishing habitation, no longer occupied by its tenant. Yet the features present the accustomed association of friendly intercourse. For one moment, we could think them asleep. The next reminds us that the blood circulates no more: the eye has lost its power of seeing, the ear of hearing, the heart of throbbing, and the limbs of moving. Quickly a thought of glory breaks in upon the mind, and we imagine the dear departed soul to be arrived at its long-wished-for rest. It is surrounded by cherubim and seraphim, and sings the song of Moses and the Lamb on Mount Zion. Amid the solemn stillness of the chamber of death, imagination hears heavenly hymns chanted by the spirits of just men made perfect. In another moment, the livid lips and sunken eye of the clay- cold corpse recall our thoughts to earth and to ourselves again. And while we think of mortality, sin, death, and the grave, we feel the prayer rise in our bosom, "Let me die the death of the righteous, and let my last end be like his!"

If there be a moment when Christ and salvation, death, judgment, heaven, and hell, appear more than ever to be momentous subjects of meditation, it is that which brings us to the side of a coffin containing the body of a departed believer.

Elizabeth's features were altered, but much of her likeness remained. Her father and mother sat at the head, her brother at the foot of the coffin. The father silently and alternately looked upon his dead child and then lifted up his eyes to heaven. A struggle for resignation to the will of God was manifest in his countenance; while the tears, rolling down his aged cheeks, at the same time declared his grief and affection. The poor mother cried and sobbed aloud, and appeared to be much overcome by the shock of separation from a daughter so justly dear to her. The weakness and infirmity of old age added a character to her sorrow which called for much tenderness and compassion.

A remarkably decent-looking woman, who had the management of the few simple though solemn ceremonies which the case required, advanced towards me, saying,—

"Sir, this is rather a sight of joy than of sorrow. Our dear friend Elizabeth finds it to be so, I have no doubt. She is beyond *all* sorrow: do you not think she is, sir?"

"After what I have known, and seen, and heard," I replied, "I feel the fullest assurance, that while her body remains here, her soul is with her Saviour in paradise. She loved him *here*, and *there* she enjoys the pleasures which are at his right hand for evermore."

"Mercy, mercy upon a poor old creature, almost broken down with age and grief!—What shall I do!—Betsy's gone. My daughter's dead—O my child! I shall never see thee more. God be merciful to me a sinner!" sobbed out the poor mother.

"That last prayer, my dear good woman," said I, "will bring you and your child together again. It is a cry that has brought thousands to glory. It brought your daughter there, and I hope it will bring you thither likewise. God will in no wise cast out any that come to him."

"My dear," said the Dairyman, breaking the long silence he had maintained, "let us trust God with our child; and let us trust him with our own selves. The Lord gave, and the Lord has taken away; blessed be the name of the Lord! We are old, and can have but a little further to travel in our journey, and then—," he could say no more

The soldier, mentioned in my last paper, reached a Bible into my hand, and said, "Perhaps, sir, you would not object to reading a chapter before we go to the church?"

I did so; it was the fourteenth of the book of Job. A sweet tranquillity prevailed while I read it. Each minute that was spent in this funeral chamber seemed to be valuable. I made a few observations on the chapter, and connected them with the case of our departed sister.

"I am but a poor soldier," said our military friend, "and have nothing of this world's goods beyond my daily subsistence; but I would not exchange my hope of salvation in the next world for all that this world could bestow without it. What is wealth without grace? Blessed be God! as I march about from one quarter to another, I still find the Lord wherever I go; and, thanks be to his holy name, he is here to-day in the midst of this company of the living and the dead. I feel that it is good to be here."

Some other persons present began to take a part in our conversation, in the course of which the life and experience of the Dairyman's daughter were brought forward in a very interesting manner. Each friend had something to relate in testimony of her gracious disposition. A young woman under twenty, who had hitherto been a very light and trifling character, appeared to be remarkably impressed by the conversation of that day; and I have since had ground to believe that Divine grace then began to influence her in the choice of that better part which shall not be taken from her.

What a contrast does such a scene as this exhibit, when compared with the dull, formal, unedifying, and often indecent manner, in which funeral parties assemble in the house of death!

As we conversed the parents revived. Our subject of discourse was delightful to their hearts. Their child seemed almost to be alive again, while we talked of her. Tearful smiles often brightened their countenances, as they heard the voice of friendship uttering their daughter's praises; or rather the praises of him who made her a vessel of mercy and an instrument of spiritual good to her family.

The time for departing to the church was now at hand.

I went to take my last look at the deceased.

There was much written on her countenance. She had evidently died with a smile. It still remained, and spoke the tranquillity of her departed soul. According to the custom of the country she was decorated with leaves and flowers in the coffin: she seemed as a bride gone forth to meet the bridegroom. These, indeed, were fading flowers, but they reminded me of that paradise whose flowers are immortal, and where her never-dying soul is at rest.

I remembered the last words which I had heard her speak, and was instantly struck with the happy thought, that "death was indeed swallowed up in victory."

As I slowly retired, I said inwardly, "Peace, my honoured sister, be to *thy* memory and to *my* soul, till we meet in a better world."

In a little time the procession formed: it was rendered the more interesting by the consideration of so many that followed the coffin being persons of a devout and spiritual character. The distance was rather more than a mile. I resolved to continue with and go before them, as they moved slowly onwards. Immediately after the body came the venerable father and mother, {87} bending with age, and weeping through much affliction of heart. Their appearance was calculated to excite every emotion of pity, love, and esteem. The other relatives followed them in order, and the several attendant friends took their places behind.

After we had advanced about a hundred yards, my meditation was unexpectedly and most agreeably interrupted by the friends who attended beginning to sing a funeral psalm. Nothing could be more sweet or solemn. The well-known effect of the open air in softening and blending the sounds of music, was here peculiarly felt. The road through which we passed was beautiful and romantic. It lay at the foot of a hill, which occasionally re-echoed the voices of the singers, and seemed to give faint replies to the notes of the mourners. The funeral knell was distinctly heard from the church tower, and greatly increased the effect which this simple and becoming service produced.

We went by several cottages: a respectful attention was universally observed as we passed; and the countenances of many proclaimed their regard for the departed young woman. The singing was regularly continued, with occasional intervals of about five minutes during our whole progress.

I cannot describe the state of my own mind as peculiarly connected with this solemn singing. I was reminded of older times and ancient piety. I wished the practice more frequent. It seems well calculated to excite and cherish devotion and religious affections.

Music, when judiciously brought into the service of religion, is one of the most delightful, and not least efficacious means of grace. I pretend not too minutely to conjecture as to the actual nature of those pleasures which, after the resurrection, the re-united body and soul will enjoy in heaven; but I can hardly persuade myself that melody and harmony will be wanting, when even the sense of hearing shall itself be glorified.

We at length arrived at the church. Looking upwards as I drew near the church, I observed a dial on the wall. The sun's declining rays directed the shadow to the evening hour. As I passed underneath this simple but solemn monitor, I was reminded of the lapse of time, the uncertainty of life, and sure approach of eternity. I thought with David, "We are strangers before thee, and sojourners, as were all our fathers; our days on earth are as a shadow, and there is none abiding."

"Lord, so teach us to number our days, that we may apply our hearts unto wisdom."

The service was heard with deep and affectionate attention. When we came to the grave, the hymn which Elizabeth had selected was sung. All was devout, simple, animating. We committed our dear sister's body to the earth, in full hope of a joyful resurrection from the dead.

Thus was the veil of separation drawn for a season. She is departed, and no more seen. But she will be seen on the right hand of her Redeemer at the last day, and will again appear to his glory, a miracle of grace and monument of mercy.

My reader, rich or poor, shall you and I appear there likewise? Are we "clothed with humility," and arrayed in the wedding garment of a redeemer's righteousness? Are we turned from idols to serve the living God? Are we sensible of our own emptiness, and therefore flying to a Saviour's fulness to obtain grace and strength? Do we indeed live in Christ, and on him, and by him, and with him? Is he our all in all? Are we "lost, and found?" "dead, and alive again?"

My *poor* reader, the Dairyman's daughter was a *poor* girl, and the child of a *poor* man. Herein thou resemblest her: but dost thou resemble *her* as she resembled Christ? Art thou made rich by faith? Hast thou a crown laid up for thee? Is thine heart set upon heavenly riches? If not, read this story once more, and then pray earnestly for like precious faith.

But if, through grace, thou dost love and serve the Redeemer that saved the Dairyman's daughter, grace, peace, and mercy be with thee! The lines are fallen unto thee in pleasant places: thou hast a goodly heritage. Press forward in duty, and wait upon the Lord, possessing thy soul in holy patience. Thou hast just been with me to the grave of a departed believer. Now "go thy way till the end be; for thou shalt rest, and stand in thy lot at the end of the days."

Elizabeth died May 30, 1801, aged 31 years.

{The Dairyman's Daughter's Grave: p89.jpg}

THE NEGRO SERVANT.

PART I.

If a map of the world, instead of being coloured, as is usual, with many gay and brilliant tints, in order to distinguish its various continents, kingdoms, and islands from each other, were to be painted with darker or brighter hues corresponding with the spiritual character of the inhabitants, what a gloomy aspect would be presented, to the eye of the *Christian* geographer, by the greater portion of the habitable globe! How dark would be the shade thus cast over the larger districts of the vast continents of Asia and America! and what a mass of gloom would characterize the African quarter of the world!

Here and there a bright spot would mark the residence of a few missionary labourers, devoting themselves to God, and scattering the rays of Christian light among the surrounding heathen; but over the greater part "the blackness of darkness" would emblematically describe the iron reign of Mohammedan superstition and Pagan idolatry.

The Christian prays that God would have "respect unto the covenant; for the dark places of the earth are full of the habitations of cruelty." He hopes to see the nations "open their eyes, and turn from darkness to light, and from the power of Satan unto God, that they may receive forgiveness of sins, and inheritance among them which are sanctified by faith."

The curse originally pronounced on the descendants of Ham has, in a variety of respects, both temporal and spiritual, been awfully fulfilled—"A servant of servants shall he be." Slavery, as well of mind as body, has been continued amongst the Africans through their generations in a manner which at once proves the truth of the Divine prediction, and yet calls aloud for the ardent prayers and active exertions of Christians in their behalf. The time will come when the heathen shall be proved to have been given to Christ "for an inheritance, and the uttermost parts of the earth for his possession." The degraded Hottentot, and the poor benighted Negro, will look from the ends of the earth unto Jesus, and be saved. "Many shall run to and fro, and knowledge shall be increased." The Redeemer "shall see of the travail of his soul, and shall be satisfied," in beholding the gathering together, not only of the outcasts of Israel that are ready to perish, but of churches and people from all the tongues, and kindreds, and nations of the earth. In the day of his appearing, the sons of Africa will vie with their brethren of the north, and the west, and the east, in resounding the praises of God their Saviour from one end of the earth to the other.

In the meantime, we rejoice in every occasional instance of the love and power of God in effecting the conversion of some, who appear as the first-fruits of that harvest which shall hereafter so fruitfully grow up, to the honour of Christ and the blessedness of his redeemed people.

The following narrative of real facts may, perhaps, illustrate the importance of the foregoing remarks.

During a residence of some years' continuance in the neighbourhood of the sea, an officer of the navy called upon me, and stated that he had just taken a lodging in the parish for his wife and children; and had a Negro, who had been three years in his service. "The lad is a deserving fellow," said the officer, "and he has a great desire to be baptized. I have promised him to ask you to do it, if you have not any objections."

"Does he know anything," replied I, "of the principles of the Christian religion?"

"Oh, yes, I am sure he does," answered the captain; "for he talks a great deal about it in the kitchen, and often gets laughed at for his pains; but he takes it all very patiently."

"Does he behave well as your servant?"

"Yes, that he does; he is as honest and civil a fellow as ever came on board ship, or lived in a house."

"Was he always so well behaved?"

"No," said the officer; "when I first had him he was often very unruly and deceitful; but for the last two years he has been quite like another creature."

"Well, sir, I shall be very glad to see him, and think it probable I shall wish to go through a course of instruction and examination; during which I shall be able to form a judgment how far it will be right to admit him to the sacrament of baptism. Can he read?"

"Yes," replied his master; "he has been taking great pains to learn to read for some time past, and can make out a chapter in the Bible pretty well, as my maid-servant informs me. He speaks English better than many of his countrymen, but you will find it a little broken. When will it be convenient that I should send him over to you?"

"To-morrow afternoon, sir, if you please."

"He shall come to you about four o'clock, and you shall see what you can make of him."

With this promise he took his leave. I felt glad of an opportunity of instructing a native of that land whose wrongs and injuries had often caused me to sigh and mourn; the more so, when I reflected *who* had been the aggressors.

At the appointed hour my Negro disciple arrived. He was a very young-looking man, with a sensible, lively, and pleasing countenance.

I desired him to sit down, and said, "Your master informs me that you wish to have some conversation with me respecting Christian baptism."

"Yes, sir; me very much wish to be a Christian," said he.

"Why do you wish so?"

"Because me know that Christian go to heaven when he die."

"How long have you had that wish?" I said.

"Ever since me heard one goot minister preach in America, two years ago."

"Where were you born?"

"In Africa. Me was very little boy when me was made slave by the white men."

"How was that?"

"Me left father and mother one day at home to go get shells by de sea-shore, and as me was stooping down to gather them up, some white sailors came out of a boat and took me away. Me never see father nor mother again."

"And what became of you then?"

"Me was put into ship, and brought to Jamaica and sold to a master, who kept me in his house to serve him some years; when, about three years ago, Captain W——, my master, dat spoke to you, bought me to be his servant on board his ship. And he be goot master; he gave me my liberty, and made me free, and me live with him ever since."

"And what thoughts had you about your soul all that time before you went to America?" I asked him.

"Me no care for my soul at all before den. No man teach me one word about my soul."

"Well, now tell me further about what happened to you in America. How came you there?"

"My master take me dere in his ship, and he stop dere one month, and den me hear de goot minister."

"And what did the minister say?"

"He said me was a great sinner."

"What! did he speak to you in particular?"

"Yes, me tink so; for dere was great many to hear him, but he tell dem all about me."

"What did he say?"

"He say about all de tings dat were in my heart."

"What things?"

"My sin, my ignorance, my know noting, my believe noting. De goot minister make me see dat me *tink* noting goot, me *do* noting goot."

"And what else did he tell you?"

"He sometime look me in de face, and say dat Jesus Christ came to die for sinners, poor black sinners as well as white sinners. Me tought dis was very goot, very goot, indeed, to do so for a wicked sinner."

"And what made you think this was all spoken to you in particular?"

"Because me sure no such wicked sinner as me in all de place. De goot minister must know me was dere."

"And what did you think of yourself while he preached about Jesus Christ?"

"Sir, me was very much afraid, when he said the wicked must be turned into hell-fire. For me felt dat me was very wicked sinner, and dat make me cry. And he talk much about de love of Christ to sinners, and dat make me cry more. And me tought me must love Jesus Christ; but me not know how, and dat make me cry again."

"Did you hear more sermons than one during that month?"

"Yes, sir; master gave me leave to go tree times, and all de times me wanted to love Jesus more, and do what Jesus said; but my heart seem sometime hard, like a stone."

"Have you ever heard any preaching since that time?"

"Never, till me hear sermon at dis church last Sunday, and den me long to be baptized in Jesus' name; for me had no Christian friends to baptize me when little child."

"And what have been your thoughts all the time since you first heard these sermons in America? Did you tell anybody what you then felt?"

"No, me speak to nobody but to God den. De goot minister say dat God hear de cry of de poor; so me cry to God, and he hear me. And me often tink about Jesus Christ, and wish to be like him."

"Can you read?"

"A little."

"Who taught you to read?"

"God teach me to read."

"What do you mean by saying so?"

"God give me desire to read, and dat make reading easy. Master give me Bible, and one sailor show me de letters: and so me learned to read by myself, with God's good help."

"And what do you read in the Bible?"

"Oh, me read all about Jesus Christ, and how he loved sinners; and wicked men killed him, and he died, and came again from de grave; and all dis for poor Negro. And it sometime make me cry, to tink that Christ love so poor Negro."

"And what do the people say about your reading, and praying, and attention to the things of God?"

"Some wicked people, dat do not love Jesus Christ, call me great fool, and Negro dog, and black hypocrite. And dat make me sometimes feel angry; but den me remember Christian must not be angry, for Jesus Christ was called ugly black names, and he was quiet as a lamb; and so den me remember Jesus Christ; and me say nothing again to dem."

I was much delighted with the simplicity and apparent sincerity of this poor Negro, and wished to ascertain what measure of light and feeling he possessed on a few leading points. St. Paul's summary of religion [97] occuring to me, I said, "Tell me what is faith? What is your faith? What do you believe about Jesus Christ, and your own soul?"

"Me believe," said he, "dat Jesus Christ came into de world to save sinners; and dough me be chief of sinners, yet Jesus will save me, dough me be only poor black Negro."

"What is your hope? What do you hope for, both as to this life and that which is to come?"

"Me hope Jesus Christ will take good care of me, and keep me from sin and harm, while me live here; and me hope, when me come to die, to go and live with him always, and never die again."

"What are your thoughts about Christian love or charity,—I mean, whom and what do you most love?"

"Me love God de Father, because he was so goot to send his Son. Me love Jesus Christ, because he love men. Me love all men, black men and white men too; for God made dem all. Me love goot Christian people, because Jesus love dem, and dey love Jesus."

Such was my first conversation with this young disciple. I rejoiced in the prospect of receiving him into the Church agreeably to his desire. I wished, however, to converse somewhat further, and inquire more minutely into his conduct; and promised to ride over and see him in a few days at his master's lodgings.

When he was gone, I thought within myself, God has indeed redeemed souls by the blood of his Son, "out of *every* kindred, and tongue, and people, and nation." If many of them for a season are devoted to earthly slavery,[98] through the cruel avarice of man, yet, blessed be God, some amongst them are, through divine grace, called to the glorious liberty of the children of God; and so are redeemed from the slavery of him who takes so many captive at his will. It is a happy thought, that "Ethiopia shall soon stretch forth her hands unto God. Sing unto God, ye kingdoms of the earth. Oh, sing praises unto the Lord."

PART II.

When we endeavour to estimate the worth of an immortal soul, we are utterly lost in the attempt. The art of spiritual computation is not governed by the same principles and rules which guide our speculations concerning earthly objects. The value of gold, silver, merchandize, food, raiment, lands, and houses, is easily regulated, by custom, convenience, or necessity. Even the more capricious and imaginary worth of a picture, medal, or statue, may be reduced to something of systematic rule. Crowns and sceptres have had their adjudged valuation; and kingdoms have been bought and sold for sums of money. But who can affix the adequate price to a human soul? "What shall it profit a man, if he shall gain the whole world, and lose his own soul? or what shall a man give in exchange for his soul?"

The principles of ordinary arithmetic all fail here; and we are constrained to say, that He alone who paid the ransom for sinners, and made the souls of men his "purchased possession," can comprehend and solve the arduous question. They are, indeed, "bought with a price," but are "not redeemed with corruptible things, as silver and gold; but with the precious blood of Christ, as of a lamb without blemish and without spot." We shall only ascertain the value of a soul, when we shall be fully able to estimate the worth of a Saviour.

Too often have we been obliged to hear what is the price which sordid, unfeeling avarice has affixed to the *body* of a poor Negro slave; let us now attempt, while we pursue the foregoing narrative, to meditate on the value which Infinite Mercy has attached to his *soul*.

Not many days after my first interview with my Negro disciple, I went from home with the design of visiting and conversing with him again at his master's house, which was situated in a part of the parish nearly four miles distant from my own. The road which I took lay over a lofty down, which commands a prospect of scenery seldom exceeded in beauty and magnificence. It gave birth to silent but instructive contemplation.

The down itself was covered with sheep, grazing on its wholesome and plentiful pasture. Here and there a shepherd's boy kept his appointed station, and watched over the flock committed to his care. I viewed it as an emblem of my own situation and employment. Adjoining the hill lay an extensive parish, wherein many souls were given me to watch over, and render an account of, at the day of the great Shepherd's appearing. The pastoral scene before me seemed to be a living parable, illustrative of my own spiritual charge. I felt a prayerful wish, that the good Shepherd, who gave His life for the sheep, might enable me to be faithful to my trust.

It occurred to me, about the same time, that my young African friend was a sheep of another more distant fold, which Christ will yet bring to hear his voice. For there shall be one fold and one Shepherd, and all nations shall be brought to acknowledge that He alone "restoreth our souls, and leadeth us in the paths of righteousness for his name's sake." On the left hand of the hill, as I advanced eastward, and immediately under its declivity, extended a beautiful tract of land intersected by a large arm of the sea, which (as the tide was fast flowing in) formed a broad lake or haven of three miles in length. Woods, villages, cottages, and churches, surrounded it in most pleasing variety of prospect. Beyond this lay a large fleet of ships of war, and not far from it another of merchantmen, both safe at anchor, and covering a tract of the sea of several miles in extent. Beyond this, again, I saw the fortifications, dockyards, and extensive public edifices of a large seaport town. The sun shone upon the windows of the buildings and the flags of the ships with great brightness, and added much to the splendour of the view.

I thought of the concerns of empires and plans of statesmen, the fate of nations and the horrors of war. Happy will be that day when He shall make wars to cease unto the end of the earth, and peace to be established in its borders.

In the meantime, let us be thankful for those vessels and instruments of defence, which, in the hands of God, preserve our country from the hand of the enemy and the fury of the destroyer. What, thought I, do we not owe to the exertions of the numerous crews on board those ships, who leave their homes to fight their country's battles and maintain its cause, whilst we sit every man under his vine and fig-tree, tasting the sweets of a tranquillity unknown to most other nations in these days of conflict and bloodshed!

On my right hand, to the south and south-east, the unbounded ocean displayed its mighty waves. It was covered with vessels of every size, sailing in all directions: some outward-bound to the most distant parts of the world; others, after a long voyage, returning home, laden with the produce of remote climes: some going forth in search of the enemy; others sailing back to port after the hard-fought engagement, and bearing the trophies of victory in the prizes which accompanied them home.

At the south-west of the spot on which I was riding extended a beautiful semicircular bay, of about nine or ten miles in circumference, bounded by high cliffs of white, red, and brown-coloured earths. Beyond this lay a range of hills, whose tops are often buried in cloudy mists, but which then appeared clear and distinct. This chain of hills, meeting with another from the north, bounds a large fruitful vale, whose fields, now ripe for harvest, proclaimed the goodness of God in the rich provision which he makes for the sons of men. It is he who prepares the corn: he crowns the year with his goodness, and his paths drop fatness. "They drop upon the pastures of the wilderness; and the little hills rejoice on every side. The pastures are clothed with flocks; the valleys also are covered over with corn; they shout for joy, they also sing."

"The roving sight
Pursues its pleasing course o'er neighbouring hills,
Of many a different form and different hue:
Bright with the rip'ning corn, or green with grass,
Or dark with clovers purple bloom."

As I looked upon the numerous ships moving before me, I remembered the words of the psalmist: "They that go down to the sea in ships, that do business in great waters; these see the works of the Lord, and his wonders in the deep. For he commandeth, and raiseth the stormy wind, which lifteth up the waves thereof. They mount up to the heaven, they go down again to the depths: their soul is melted because of trouble. They reel to and fro, and stagger like a drunken man, and are at their wits end. Then they cry unto the Lord in their trouble, and he bringeth them out of their distresses. He maketh the storm a calm, so that the waves thereof are still. Then are they glad because they be quiet; so he bringeth them unto their desired haven. Oh that men would praise the Lord for his goodness, and for his wonderful works to the children of men!" (Ps. cvii. 23-31.)

The Negro servant then occurred to my mind. Perhaps, thought I, some of these ships are bound to Africa, in quest of that most infamous object of merchandise, a cargo of black slaves. Inhuman traffic for a nation that bears the name of Christian! Perhaps these very waves, that are now dashing on the rocks at the foot of this hill, have, on the shores of Africa, borne witness to the horrors of forced separation between wives and husbands, parents and children, torn asunder by merciless men, whose hearts have been hardened against the common feeling of humanity by long custom in this cruel trade. "Blessed are the merciful; for they shall obtain mercy." When shall the endeavours of *that* truly Christian *friend* of the oppressed Negro be crowned with success, in the abolition of this wicked and disgraceful traffic?[103]

As I pursued the meditations which this magnificent and varied scenery excited in my mind, I approached the edge of a tremendous perpendicular cliff, with which the down terminates. I dismounted from my horse, and tied it to a bush. The breaking of the waves against the foot of the cliff at so great a distance beneath me, produced an incessant and pleasing murmur. The sea-gulls were flying between the top of the cliff where I stood and the rocks below, attending upon their nests, built in the holes of the cliff. The whole scene in every direction was grand and impressive; it was suitable to devotion. The Creator appeared in the works of his creation, and called upon the creatures to honour and adore. To the believer, this exercise is doubly delightful. He possesses a right to the enjoyment of nature and providence, as well as to the privileges of grace. His title-deed runs thus: "All things are yours; whether Paul, or Apollos, or Cephas, or the world, or life, or death, or things present, or things to come; all are yours; and ye are Christ's; and Christ is God's."

I cast my eye downwards a little to the left towards a small cove, the shore of which consists of fine hard sand. It is surrounded by fragments of rock, chalk-cliffs, and steep banks of broken earth. Shut out from human intercourse and dwellings, it seems formed for retirement and contemplation. On one of these rocks I unexpectedly observed a man sitting with a book which he was reading. The place was near two hundred yards perpendicularly below me, but I soon discovered by his dress, and by the black colour of his features contrasted with the white rocks beside him, that it was no other than my Negro disciple, with, as I doubted not, a Bible in his hand. I rejoiced at this unlooked-for opportunity of meeting him in so solitary and interesting a situation. I descended a steep bank, winding by a kind of rude staircase, formed by fishermen and shepherds' boys, in the side of the cliff down to the shore.

He was intent on his book, and did not perceive me till I approached very near to him.

"William, is that you?"

"Ah, massa! me very glad to see you. How came massa into dis place? Me tought nobody here, but only God and me."

"I was coming to your master's house to see you, and rode round by this way for the sake of the prospect. I often come here in fine weather, to look at the sea and shipping. Is that your Bible?"

"Yes, sir;{105} dis my dear goot Bible."

"I am glad," said I, "to see you so well employed. It is a good sign, William."

"Yes, massa, a sign that God is goot to me; but me never goot to God."

"How so?"

"Me never tank him enough; me never pray to him enough: me never remember enough who give me all dese goot tings. Massa, me afraid my heart is very bat. Me wish me was like you."

"Like me, William? Why, you are like me, a poor helpless sinner, that must, as well as yourself, perish in his sins, unless God, of his infinite mercy and grace, pluck him as a brand from the burning, and make him an instance of distinguishing love and favour. There is no difference; we have both come short of the glory of God: all have sinned."

"No, me not like you, massa; me tink nobody like me,—nobody feel such a heart as me."

"Yes, William, your feelings, I am persuaded, are like those of every truly convinced soul, who sees the exceeding sinfulness of sin, and the greatness of the price which Christ Jesus paid for the sinner's ransom. You can say, in the words of the hymn,—

'I the chief of sinners am,
But Jesus died for me.'"

"O yes, sir, me believe that Jesus died for poor Negro. What would become of poor wicked Negro, if Christ no die for him? But he die for de chief of sinners, and dat make my heart sometimes quite glad."

"What part of the Bible were you reading, William?"

"Me read how de man upon de cross spoke to Christ, and Christ spoke to him. Now dat man's prayer just do for me; 'Lord, remember me.' Lord, remember poor Negro sinner: dis is my prayer every morning, and sometimes at night too; when me cannot tink of many words, den me say de same again; Lord, remember poor Negro sinner."

"And be sure, William, the Lord hears that prayer. He pardoned and accepted the thief upon the cross, and he will not reject you; he will in no wise cast out any that come to him."

"No, sir, I believe it; but dere is so much sin in my heart, it makes me afraid and sorry. Massa, do you see dese limpets,{107} how fast dey stick to de rocks here? Just so, sin sticks fast to my heart."

"It may be so, William; but take another comparison: do you cleave to Jesus Christ, by faith in his death and righteousness, as those limpets cleave to the rock, and neither seas nor storms shall separate you from his love."

"Dat is just what me want."

"Tell me, William, is not that very sin which you speak of a burden to you? You do not love it; you would be glad to obtain strength against it, and to be freed from it; would you not?"

"O yes; me give all dis world, if me had it, to be without sin!"

"Come then, and welcome, to Jesus Christ, my brother; his blood cleanseth from all sin. He gave himself as a ransom for sinners. He hath borne our grief, and carried our sorrows. He was wounded for our transgressions; he was bruised for our iniquities; the chastisement of our peace was upon him, and with his stripes we are healed. The Lord hath laid on him the iniquity of us all. Come, freely come to Jesus, the Saviour of sinners."

"Yes, massa," said the poor fellow, weeping, "me will come: but me come very slow; very slow, massa: me want to run, me want to fly. Jesus is very goot to poor Negro, to send you to tell him all dis."

"But this is not the first time you have heard these truths!"

"No, sir; dey have been comfort to my soul many times, since me hear goot minister preach in America, as me tell you last week at your house."

"Well, now I hope, William, that since God has been so graciously pleased to open your eyes, and affect your mind with such a great sense of his goodness in giving his Son to die for your sake; I hope that you do your endeavour to keep his commandments: I hope you strive to behave well to your master and mistress, and fellow-servants. He that is a Christian inwardly will be a Christian outwardly; he that truly and savingly believes in Christ, will show his faith by his works, as the apostle says. Is it not so, William?"

"Yes, sir; me want to do so. Me want to be faithful. Me sorry to tink how bat servant me was before de goot tings of Jesus Christ come to my heart. Me wish to do well to my massa, when he see me and when he not see; for me know God always see me. Me know dat if me sin against mine own massa, me sin against God, and God be very angry with me. Beside, how can me love Christ if me do not what Christ tell me? Me love my fellow-servants, dough, as I tell you before, dey do not much love me; and I pray God to bless dem. And when dey say bat tings, and try to make me angry, den me tink, if Jesus Christ were in poor Negro's place, he would not revile and answer again with bat words and temper, but he say little and pray much. And so den me say noting at all, but pray to God to forgive dem."

The more I conversed with this African convert, the more satisfactory were the evidences of his mind being spiritually enlightened, and his heart effectually wrought upon by the grace of God.

The circumstances of the place in which we met together contributed much to the interesting effect which the conversation produced on my mind. The little cove or bay was beautiful in the extreme. The air was calm and serene. The sun shone, but we were sheltered from its rays by the cliffs. One of these was stupendously lofty and large. It was white as snow; its summit hung directly over our heads. The sea-fowls were flying around it. Its whiteness was occasionally chequered with dark green masses of samphire, which grew there. On the other side, and behind us, was a more gradual declivity of many-coloured earths, interspersed with green patches of grass and bushes, and little streams of water trickling down the bank, and mingling with the sea at the bottom. At our feet the waves were advancing over shelves of rocks covered with a great variety of sea-weeds, which swam in little fragments, and displayed much beauty and elegance of form as they were successively thrown upon the sand.

Ships of war and commerce were seen at different distances. Fishermen were plying their trade in boats nearer the shore. The noise of the flowing tide, combined with the voices of the sea-gulls over our heads, and now and then a distant gun fired from the ships as they passed along, added much to the peculiar sensations to which the scene gave birth. Occasionally the striking of oars upon the waves, accompanied by the boatmen's song, met the ear. The sheep aloft upon the down sometimes mingled their bleatings with the other sounds. Thus all nature seemed to unite in impressing an attentive observer's heart with affecting thoughts.

I remained for a considerable time in conversation with the Negro, finding that his master was gone from home for the day, and had given him liberty for some hours. I spoke to him on the nature, duty, and privilege of Christian baptism; pointed out to him, from a prayer-book which I had with me, the clear and scriptural principles of our own church upon that head; and found that he was very desirous of conforming to them. He appeared to me to be well qualified for receiving that sacramental pledge of his Redeemer's love; and I rejoiced in the prospect of beholding him no longer a "stranger and foreigner, but a fellow-citizen with the saints, and of the household of God."

"God," said I to him, "has promised to 'sprinkle many nations,' not only with the waters of baptism, but also with the dews of his heavenly grace. He says he will not only 'pour water on him that is thirsty,' but, 'I will pour my Spirit upon thy seed, and my blessing upon thine offspring.'"

"Yes, massa," said he, "he can make me to be clean in heart, and of a right Spirit; he can purge me with hyssop, and I shall be clean; he can wash me, and I shall be whiter dan snow."

"May God give you these blessings, and confirm you in every good gift!"

I was much pleased with the affectionate manner in which he spoke of his parents, from whom he had been stolen in his childhood; and his wishes that God might direct them by some means to the knowledge of the Saviour.

"Who knows," I said, "but some of these ships may be carrying a missionary to the country where they live, to declare the good news of salvation to your countrymen, and to your own dear parents in particular, if they are yet alive!"

"Oh, my dear fader and moder! My dear gracious Saviour," exclaimed he, leaping from the ground as he spoke, "if dou wilt but save deir souls, and tell dem what dou hast done for sinner; but—"

He stopped, and seemed much affected.

"My friend," said I, "I will now pray with you, for your own soul, and for those of your parents also."

"Do, massa; dat is very good and kind: do pray for poor Negro souls here and everywhere."

This was a new and solemn "house of prayer." The sea-sand was our floor, the heavens were our roof, the cliffs, the rocks, the hills, and the waves, formed the walls of our chamber. It was not, indeed, a "place where prayer was wont to be made;" but for this once it became a hallowed spot: it will by me ever be remembered as such. The presence of God was there. I prayed: the Negro wept. His heart was full. I felt with him, and could not but weep likewise.

The last day will show whether our tears were not the tears of sincerity and Christian love.

It was time for my return. I leaned upon his arm as we ascended the steep cliff on my way back to my horse, which I had left at the top of the hill. Humility and thankfulness were marked in his countenance. I leaned upon his arm with the feelings of a *brother*. It was a relationship I was happy to own. I took him by the hand at parting, appointed one more interview previous to the day of baptizing him, and bade him farewell for the present.

"God bless you, my dear massa!"

"And you, my fellow-Christian, for ever and ever!"

PART III.

The interesting and affecting conversation which I had with the Negro servant produced a sensation not easy to be expressed. As I returned home, I was led into meditation on the singular clearness and beauty of those evidences of faith and conversion of heart to God, which I had just seen and heard. How plainly, I thought, it appears that salvation is freely "by grace through faith; and that not of ourselves; it is the gift of God; not of works, lest any man should boast." What but the Holy Spirit, who is the author and giver of the life of grace, could have wrought such a change from the once dark, perverse, and ignorant heathen, to this now convinced, enlightened, humble, and believing Christian! How manifestly is the uncontrolled sovereignty of the Divine will exercised in the calling and translating of sinners from darkness to light! What a lesson may the nominal Christian of a civilized country sometimes learn from the simple, sincere religion of a converted heathen!

I afterwards made particular inquiry into this young man's domestic and general deportment. Everything I heard was satisfactory, nor could I entertain a doubt respecting the consistency of his conduct and character. I had some further conversations with him, in the course of which I pursued such a plan of scriptural instruction and examination as I conceived to be the most suitable to his progressive state of mind. He improved much in reading, carried his Bible constantly with him, and took every opportunity which his duty to his master's service would allow for perusing it. I have frequently had occasion to observe that amongst the truly religious poor, who have not had the advantage of being taught to read in early youth, a concern about the soul and a desire to know the word of God, have proved effectual motives for their learning to read with great ease and advantage to themselves and others. It was strikingly so in the present case.

I had, for a considerable time, been accustomed to meet some serious persons once a week, in a cottage at no great distance from the house where he lived, for the purpose of religious conversation, instruction, and prayer. Having found these occasions remarkably useful and interesting, I thought it would be very desirable to take the Negro there, in order that there might be other witnesses to the simplicity and sincerity of real Christianity, as exhibited in the character of this promising young convert. I hoped it might prove an eminent mean of grace to excite and quicken the spirit of prayer and praise amongst some of my parishioners, over whose spiritual progress I was anxiously watching.

I accordingly obtained his master's leave that he should attend me to one of my cottage assemblies. His master, who was thoroughly convinced of the extraordinary change, in conduct and disposition, which religion had produced in his servant, was pleased with my attention to him, and always spoke well of his behaviour.

I set out on the day appointed for the interview. The cottage at which we usually assembled was nearly four miles distant from my own residence. My road lay along the foot of the hill mentioned in my last account of the Negro, from the summit of which so luxuriant a prospect was seen. On my right hand the steep acclivity of the hill intercepted all prospect, except that of numerous sheep feeding on its rich and plentiful produce. Here and there the nearly perpendicular side of a chalk-pit varied the surface of the hill, contrasting a dazzling white to the sober green of the surrounding bank.

On the left hand, at the distance of nearly half a mile, the tide flowed from the sea into a lake or haven of a considerable length and breadth. At one end of it, fishing and pilot vessels lay at anchor; at the other appeared the parish church, amongst the adjoining woods and fields. The bells were ringing; a gently swelling sound was brought along the surface of the water, and an echo returned from a prominent part of the hill beneath which I was riding. The whole scene was delightful.

I passed some rural and beautifully situated cottages, which seemed to be formed as fit residences for peace and tranquillity; each was surrounded by a garden, and each had a little orchard or field adjacent, where the husbandman's cow enjoyed her own pasture, and at the same time prepared rich provision for her owner's family. Such was the wise and considerate allotment which the landlords and the farmers had *here* made for the labouring poor. The wholesome vegetable, the medicinal herb, and the sweet-scented flower, intermingled as they grew around these little dwellings, and reminded me, as I looked upon them, how comfortable is the lot of the industrious poor, whose hearts have learned the lesson of gratitude in the school of heavenly wisdom. For them as mercifully as for their richest neighbour, the sun shines, the rain descends, the earth brings forth her increase, the flower blossoms, the bird sings. Their wants are few, and contentment makes them less. How great the blessing of being poor in this world, but rich in faith and a chosen inheritance in a better!

I knew that this was the character of some whose humble but neat and cleanly cottages I passed. A few such features in the prospect rendered it most lovely. Peace be to their memory, both as pilgrims and strangers here, and as ransomed souls whom I hope to meet in glory hereafter!

The house to which I was travelling was situated at the corner of an oak wood, which screened it both from the burning heat of summer suns and the heavy blasts of winter south-west storms. As I approached it, I saw my friend the Negro sitting under a tree, and waiting my arrival. He held in his hand a little tract which I had given him; his Bible lay on the ground. He rose with much cheerfulness, saying—

"Ah, massa, me very glad to see you; me tink you long time coming."

"William, I hope you are well. I am going to take you with me to a few of my friends, who, I trust, are truly sincere in their religious pursuits. We meet every Wednesday evening for conversation about the things that belong to our everlasting peace, and I am sure you will be a welcome visitor."

"Massa, me not goot enough to be with such goot people. Me great sinner; dey be goot Christian."

"If you were to ask them, William, they would each tell you they were worse than others. Many of them were once, and that not very long ago, living in an openly sinful manner, ignorant of God, and the enemies of Jesus Christ by thought and deed. But divine grace stopped them in their wicked course, and subdued their hearts to the love and obedience of him and his gospel. You will only meet a company of poor fellow-sinners, who love to speak and sing the praises of redeeming love; and I am sure, William, that is a song in which you will be willing to join them."

"O yes, sir! dat song just do for poor Negro."

By this time we had arrived at the cottage garden gate. Several well- known faces appeared in and near the house, and the smile of affection welcomed us as we entered. It was known that the Negro was to visit the little society this evening, and satisfaction beamed on every countenance, as I took him by the hand and introduced him among them, saying, "I have brought a brother from Africa to see you, my friends. Bid him welcome in the name of our Lord Jesus Christ."

"Sir," said an humble and pious labourer, whose heart and tongue always overflowed with Christian kindness, "we are at all times glad to see our dear minister, but especially so to-day in such company as you have brought with you. We have heard how merciful the Lord has been to him. Give me your hand, good friend (turning to the Negro). God be with you, here and everywhere; and blessed be his holy name for calling sinners, as I hope he has done you and me, to love and serve him for his mercy's sake."

Each one greeted him as he came into the house, and some addressed him in very kind and impressive language.

"Massa," said he, "me not know what to say to all dese goot friends; me tink dis look a little like heaven upon earth."

He then, with tears in his eyes—which, almost before he spoke, brought responsive drops into those of many present—said, "Goot friends and bredren in Christ Jesus, God bless you all, and bring you to heaven at de last."

It was my stated custom, when I met to converse with these cottagers, to begin with prayer and reading a portion of the Scriptures.

When this was ended, I told the people present that the providence of God had placed this young man for a time under my ministry; and that, finding him seriously disposed, and believing him to be very sincere in his religious profession, I had resolved on baptizing him, agreeably to his own wishes. I added, that I had now brought him with me to join in Christian conversation with us; for, as in olden times they that feared the Lord spake often one to another, in testimony that they thought upon his name (Mal. iii. 16), so I hoped we were fulfilling a Christian and brotherly duty in thus assembling for mutual edification.

Addressing myself to the Negro, I said, "William, tell me who made you."

"God, de goot Fader."

"Who redeemed you?"

"Jesus, his dear Son, who died for me."

"Who sanctified you?"

"The Holy Ghost, who teach me to know de goot Fader, and his dear Son Jesus."

"What was your state by nature?"

"Me wicked sinner; me know noting but sin, me do noting but sin; my soul more black dan my body."

"Has any change taken place in you since then?"

"Me hope so, massa; but me sometime afraid no."

"If you are changed, who changed you?"

"God de goot Fader, Jesus his dear Son, and God de Holy Spirit."

"How was any change brought about in you?"

"God make me a slave when me was young little boy."

"How, William? would you say God made you a slave?"

"No, massa, no: me mean, God let me be made slave by white men, to do me goot."

"How to do you good?"

"He take me from de land of darkness, and bring me to de land of light."

"Which do you call the land of light? the West India Islands?"

"No, massa; dey be de land of Providence, but America be de land of light to me; for dere me first hear goot minister preach. And now dis place where I am now is de land of more light; for here you teach me more and more how goot Jesus is to sinners."

"What does the blood of Christ do?"

"It cleanse from all sin; and so me hope from my sin."

"Are then all men cleansed from sin by his blood?"

"O no, massa."

"Who are cleansed and saved?"

"Dose dat have faith in him."

"Can you prove that out of the Bible?"

"Yes, sir: 'He dat believeth on de Son hath everlasting life; and he dat believeth not de Son shall not see life, but de wrath of God abideth on him'" (John iii. 36).

"What is it to have faith?"

"Me suppose dat it is to tink much about Jesus Christ, to love him much, to believe all he says to be true, to pray to him very much; and when me feel very weak and very sinful, to tink dat he is very strong and very goot, and all dat for my sake."

"And have you such a faith as you describe?"

"Oh, massa! me tink sometimes me have no faith at all."

"Why so, William?"

"When me want to tink about Jesus Christ, my mind run about after oder tings; when me want to love him, my heart soon quite cold; when me want to believe all to be true what he says to sinners, me den tink it is not true for me; when me want to pray, de devil put bat, very bat thoughts into me; and me never tank Christ enough. Now all dis make me sometimes afraid I have no faith."

I observed a very earnest glow of attention and fellow-feeling in some countenances present, as he spoke these words I then said—

"I think, William, I can prove that you have faith, notwithstanding your fears to the contrary. Answer me a few more questions.

"Did you begin to think yourself a great sinner, and to feel the want of a Saviour, of your own self, and by your own thoughts and doings?"

"O no; it came to me when me tink noting about it, and seek noting about it."

"Who sent the good minister in America to awaken your soul by his preaching?"

"God, very certainly."

"Who then began the work of serious thought in your mind?"

"De goot God; me could not do it of myself, me sure of dat."

"Do you not think that Jesus Christ and his salvation are the one thing most needful and most desirable?"

"Oh yes, me quite sure of dat."

"Do you not believe that he is able to save you?"

"Yes, he is able to save to de uttermost."

"Do you think he is not willing to save you?"

"Me dare not say dat. He is so goot, so merciful, so kind, to say he will in no wise cast out any dat come to him."

"Do you wish, and desire, and strive to keep his commandments?"

"Yes, massa, because me love him, and dat make me want to do as he say."

"Are you willing to suffer for his sake, if God should call you to do so?"

"Me do tink me could die for de love of him: he not tink it too much to die for wicked sinner; why should wicked sinner tink it much to die for so goot and righteous a Saviour?"

"I think and hope I may say to you, William, 'Thy faith hath made thee whole.'"

Thus ended my examination for the present. The other friends who were in the house listened with the most affectionate anxiety to all that passed. One of them observed, not without evident emotion—

"I see, sir, that though some men are white and some are black, true Christianity is all of one colour. My own heart has gone with this good man, every word he has spoken."

"And so has mine," gently re-echoed from every part of the room.

After some time passed in more general conversation on the subject of the Negro's history, I said, "Let us now praise God for the rich and unspeakable gift of his grace, and sing the hymn of redeeming love—

'Now begin the heavenly theme,
Sing aloud in Jesus' name,'" &c.

Which was accordingly done. Whatever might be the merit of the natural voices, it was evident there was spiritual melody in all their hearts.

The Negro was not much used to our way of singing, yet joined with great earnestness and affection, that showed how truly he felt what he uttered. When the fifth verse was ended—

"Nothing brought him from above,
Nothing but redeeming love"—

he repeated the words, almost unconscious where he was—
"No, noting, noting but redeeming love, bring him down to poor William; noting but redeeming love."
The following verses were added and sung by way of conclusion:—

See, a stranger comes to view,
Though he's black,[121] he's comely too
Comes to join the choirs above,
Singing of redeeming love.

Welcome, Negro, welcome here,
Banish doubt and banish fear;
You, who Christ's salvation prove,
Praise and bless redeeming love.

I concluded with some remarks on the nature of salvation by grace, exhorting all present to press forward in the heavenly journey. It was an evening the circumstances of which, had they never been recorded on earth, were yet, doubtless, registered in the book of remembrance above.

I then fixed the day for the baptism of the Negro, and so took leave of my little affectionate circle.

The moon shone bright as I returned home, and was beautifully reflected from the waters of the lake; harmony and repose characterized the scene. I had just been uniting in the praises of the God of grace and providence; and now the God of nature demanded a fresh tribute of thanksgiving for the beauties and comforts of creation; as David sang, "When I consider thy heavens, the work of thy fingers, the moon and the stars, which thou hast ordained; what is man, that thou art mindful of him? and the son of man, that thou visitest him?"

In a few days the Negro was baptized, and not long after went on a voyage with his master.

Since that time I have not been able to hear any tidings of him. Whether he yet wanders as a pilgrim in this lower world, or whether he has joined the heavenly choir in the song of "redeeming love" in glory, I know not. This I do know, he was a monument to the Lord's praise. He bore the impression of the Saviour's image on his heart, and exhibited the marks of divine grace in his life and conversation, with singular simplicity and unfeigned sincerity.

Give to God the glory.

THE YOUNG COTTAGER.

PART I.

When a serious Christian turns his attention to the barren state of the wilderness through which he is travelling, frequently must he heave a sigh for the sins and sorrows of his fellow-mortals. The renewed heart thirsts with holy desire that the Paradise which was lost through Adam may be fully regained in Christ. But the overflowings of sin within and without, the contempt of sacred institutions, the carelessness of soul, the pride of unbelief, the eagerness of sensual appetite, the ambition for worldly greatness, and the deep-rooted enmity of the carnal heart against God: these things are as "the fiery serpents, and scorpions, and drought," which distress his soul, as he journeys through "that great and terrible wilderness."

Sometimes, like a solitary pilgrim, he weeps in secret places, and rivers of water run down his eyes, because men keep not the law of God.

Occasionally he meets with a few fellow-travellers whose spirit is congenial with his own, and with whom he can take "sweet counsel together." They comfort and strengthen each other by the way. Each can relate something of the mercies of his God, and how kindly they have been dealt with, as they travelled onwards. The dreariness of the path is thus beguiled, and now and then, for a while, happy experiences of the divine consolation cheer their souls; "the wilderness and the solitary place are glad for them; the desert rejoices and blossoms as the rose."

But even at the very time when the Christian is taught to feel the peace of God which passeth all understanding, to trust that he is personally interested in the blessings of salvation, and to believe that God will promote his own glory by glorifying the penitent sinner; yet sorrows will mingle with his comforts, and he will rejoice, not without trembling, when he reflects on the state of other men. The anxieties connected with earthly relations are all alive in his soul, and, through the operation of the Spirit of God, become sanctified principles and motives for action. As the husband and father of a family; as the neighbour of the poor, the ignorant, the wicked, and the wretched; above all, as the spiritual overseer of the flock, if such be his holy calling, the heart which has been taught to feel for its own case will abundantly feel for others.

But when he attempts to devise means in order to stem the torrent of iniquity, to instruct the ignorant, and to convert the sinner from the error of his way, he cannot help crying out, "Who is sufficient for these things?" Unbelief passes over the question, and trembles. But faith quickly revives the inquirer with the cheerful assurance that "our sufficiency is of God," and saith, "Commit thy way unto the Lord, and he shall bring it to pass."

When he is thus affectionately engaged for the good of mankind, he will become seriously impressed with the necessity of early attentions to the young in particular. Many around him are grown gray-headed in sin, and give but little prospect of amendment. Many of the parents and heads of families are so eagerly busied in the profits, pleasures, and occupations of the world, that they heed not the warning voice of their instructor. Many of their elder children are launching out into life, headstrong, unruly, "earthly, sensual, devilish;" they likewise treat the wisdom of God as if it were foolishness. But, under these discouragements, we may often turn with hope to the very young, to the little ones of the flock, and endeavour to teach them to sing hosannas to the Son of David, before their minds are wholly absorbed in the world and its allurements. We may trust that a blessing shall attend such labours, if undertaken in faith and simplicity, and that some at least of our youthful disciples, like Josiah, while they are yet young, may begin to seek after the God of their fathers.

Such an employment, especially when blessed by any actual instances of real good produced, enlivens the mind with hope, and fills it with gratitude. We are thence led to trust that the next generation may become more fruitful unto God than the present, and the Church of Christ be replenished with many such as have been called into the vineyard "early in the morning." And should our endeavours for a length of time apparently fail of success, yet we ought not to despair. Early impressions and convictions of conscience have sometimes lain dormant for years, and at last revived into gracious existence and maturity. It was not said in vain, "Train up a child in the way he should go, and when he is old he will not depart from it."

What a gratifying occupation it is to an affectionate mind, even in a way of nature, to walk through the fields, and lead a little child by the hand, enjoying its infantine prattle, and striving to improve the time by some kind word of instruction! I wish that every Christian pilgrim in the way of grace, as he walks through the Lord's pastures, would try to lead at least one little child by the hand; and perhaps, whilst he is endeavouring to guide and preserve his young and feeble companion, the Lord will recompense him double for all his cares by comforting his own heart in the attempt. The experiment is worth the trial. It is supported by this recollection,—"The Lord will come with strong hand, and his arm shall rule for him; behold, his reward is with him, and his work before him. He shall feed his flock like a shepherd; he shall gather the lambs with his arm, and carry them in his bosom, and *shall gently lead those that are with young.*"

I shall plead no further apology for introducing to the notice of my readers a few particulars relative to a young female cottager, whose memory is particularly endeared to me from the circumstance of her being, so far as I can trace or discover, my first-born spiritual child in the ministry of the gospel. She was certainly the first, of whose conversion to God, under my own pastoral instruction, I can speak with precision and assurance.

Every parent of a family knows that there is a very interesting emotion of heart connected with the birth of his first-born child. Energies and affections, to which the mind has hitherto been almost a stranger, begin to unfold themselves and expand into active existence when he first is hailed as a father. But may not the spiritual father be allowed the possession and indulgence of a similar sensation in his connection with the children whom the Lord gives him, as begotten through the ministry of the word of life! If the first-born child in nature be received as a new and acceptable blessing, how much more so the first-born child in grace! I claim this privilege, and crave permission, in writing what follows, to erect a monumental record, sacred to the memory of a dear little child, who, I trust, will at the last day prove my crown of rejoicing.

Jane S— was the daughter of poor parents, in the village where it pleased God first to cast my lot in the ministry. My acquaintance with her commenced when she was twelve years of age by her weekly attendance at my house amongst a number of children whom I invited and regularly instructed every Saturday afternoon.

They used to read, repeat catechisms, psalms, hymns, and portions of Scripture. I accustomed them also to pass a kind of free conversational examination, according to their age and ability, in those subjects by which I hoped to see them made wise unto salvation.

On the summer evenings I frequently used to assemble this little group out of doors in my garden, sitting under the shade of some trees, which protected us from the heat of the sun; from hence a scene appeared, which rendered my occupation the more interesting. For adjoining the spot where we sat, and only separated from us by a fence, was the churchyard, surrounded with beautiful prospects in every direction.

There lay the mortal remains of thousands, who, from age to age, in their different generations, had been successively committed to the grave,—"earth to earth, ashes to ashes, dust to dust." Here the once famed ancestors of the rich, and the less known forefathers of the poor lay mingling their dust together, and alike waiting the resurrection from the dead.

I had not far to look for subjects of warning and exhortation suitable to my little flock of lambs that I was feeding. I could point to the heaving sods that marked the different graves and separated them from each other, and tell my pupils that, young as they were, none of them were too young to die; and that probably more than half of the bodies which were buried there were those of little children. I hence took occasion to speak of the nature and value of a soul, and to ask them where they expected their souls to go when they departed hence and were no more seen on earth.

I told them who was "the resurrection and the life," and who alone could take away the sting of death. I used to remind them that the hour was "coming in the which all that are in the graves shall hear His voice, and shall come forth: they that have done good, unto the resurrection of life; and they that have done evil, unto the resurrection of damnation." I often availed myself of these opportunities to call to their recollection the more recent deaths of their own relatives that lay buried so near us. Some had lost a parent, others a brother or sister; some perhaps had lost all these, and were committed to the mercy of their neighbours as fatherless or motherless orphans. Such circumstances were occasionally useful to excite tender emotions, favourable to serious impressions.

Sometimes I sent the children to the various stones which stood at the head of the graves, and bid them learn the epitaphs inscribed upon them. I took pleasure in seeing the little ones thus dispersed in the churchyard, each committing to memory a few verses written in commemoration of the departed. They would soon accomplish the desired object, and eagerly return to me ambitious to repeat their task.

Thus my churchyard became a book of instruction, and every grave-stone a leaf of edification for my young disciples.

The church itself stood in the midst of the ground. It was a spacious antique structure. Within those very walls I first proclaimed the message of God to sinners. As these children surrounded me, I sometimes pointed to the church, spoke to them of the nature of public worship, the value of the Sabbath, the duty of regular attendance on its services, and urged their serious attention to the means of grace. I showed them the sad state of many countries, where neither churches nor Bibles were known, and the no less melancholy condition of multitudes at home, who sinfully neglect worship and slight the word of God. I thus tried to make them sensible of their own favours and privileges.

Neither was I at a loss for another class of objects around me from which I could draw useful instruction; for many of the beauties of created nature appealed in view.

Eastward of us extended a large river or lake of sea-water, chiefly formed by the tide, and nearly enclosed by land. Beyond this was a fine bay and road for ships, filled with vessels of every size, from the small sloop or cutter to the first-rate man-of-war. On the right hand of the haven rose a hill of peculiarly beautiful form and considerable height. Its verdure was very rich, and many hundred sheep graced upon its sides and summit. From the opposite shore of the same water a large sloping extent of bank was diversified with fields, woods, hedges, and cottages. At its extremity stood, close to the edge of the sea itself, the remains of the tower of an ancient church, still preserved as a sea-mark. Far beyond the bay, a very distant shore was observable, and land beyond it; trees, towns, and other buildings appeared, more especially when gilded by the reflected rays of the sun.

To the south-westward of the garden was another down, covered also with flocks of sheep, and a portion of it fringed with trees. At the foot of this hill lay the village, a part of which gradually ascended to the rising ground on which the church stood.

From the intermixture of houses with gardens, orchards, and trees, it presented a very pleasing aspect. Several fields adjoined the garden on the east and north, where a number of cattle were pasturing. My own little shrubberies and flower-beds variegated the view, and recompensed my toil in rearing them, as well by their beauty as their fragrance.

Had the sweet psalmist of Israel sat in this spot, he would have glorified God the Creator by descanting on these his handiworks. I cannot write psalms like David, but I wish, in my own poor way, to praise the Lord for his goodness, and to show forth his wonderful works to the children of men. But had David been also surrounded with a troop of young scholars in such a situation, he would once more have said, "Out of the mouths of babes and sucklings hast thou ordained strength."

I love to retrace these scenes; they are past, but the recollection is sweet.

I love to retrace them, for they bring to my mind many former mercies, which ought not, for the Lord's sake, to be forgotten.

I love to retrace them, for they reassure me that, in the course of that private ministerial occupation, God was pleased to give me so valuable a fruit of my labours.

Little Jane used constantly to appear on these weekly seasons of instruction. I made no very particular observations concerning her during the first twelve months or more after her commencement of attendance. She was not then remarkable for any peculiar attainment. On the whole, I used to think her rather more slow of apprehension than most of her companions. She usually repeated her tasks correctly, but was seldom able to make answers to questions for which she was not previously prepared with replies—a kind of extempore examination, in which some of the children excelled. Her countenance was not engaging; her eye discovered no remarkable liveliness. She read tolerably well, took pains, and improved in it.

Mildness and quietness marked her general demeanour. She was very constant in her attendance on public worship at the church, as well as on my Saturday instruction at home. But, generally speaking, she was little noticed, except for her regular and orderly conduct. Had I then been asked of which of my young scholars I had formed the most favourable opinion, poor Jane might have been altogether omitted in the list.

How little do we oftentimes know what God is doing in other people's hearts! What poor calculators and judges we frequently prove till he opens our eyes! His thoughts are not our thoughts; neither our ways his ways.

Once, indeed, during the latter part of that year, I was struck with her ready attention to my wishes. I had, agreeably to the plan above mentioned, sent her into the churchyard to commit to memory an epitaph which I admired. On her return she told me that, in addition to what I desired, she had also learned another, which was inscribed on an adjoining stone, adding, that she thought it a very pretty one.

I thought so too, and perhaps my readers will be of the same opinion. Little Jane, though dead, yet shall speak. While I transcribe the lines, I can powerfully imagine that I hear her voice repeating them. The idea is exceedingly gratifying to me.

EPITAPH ON MRS. A. B.

Forgive, blest shade, the tributary tear
    That mourns a thy exit from a world like this;
Forgive the wish that would have kept thee here,
    And stayed thy progress to the seats of bliss.

No more confined to grovelling scenes of night,
    No more a tenant pent in mortal clay;

Now should we rather hail thy glorious flight,
    And trace thy journey to the realms of day.

The above was her appointed task; and the other, which she voluntarily learned and spoke of with pleasure, is this:—

EPITAPH ON THE STONE ADJOINING.

It must be so—Our father Adam's fall,
And disobedience, brought this lot on all.
All die in him—But, hopeless should we be,
Blest Revelation! were it not for thee.
Hail, glorious Gospel! heavenly light, whereby
We live with comfort, and with comfort die;
And view, beyond this gloomy scene the tomb
A life of endless happiness to come.

I afterwards discovered that the sentiment expressed in the latter epitaph had much affected her, but at the period of this little incident I knew nothing of her mind; I had comparatively overlooked her. I have often been sorry for it since. Conscience seemed to rebuke me when I afterwards discovered what the Lord had been doing for her soul, as if I had neglected her, yet it was not done designedly. She was unknown to us all, except that, as I since found out, her regularity and abstinence from the sins and follies of her young equals in age and station brought upon her many taunts and jeers from others, which she bore very meekly; but at that time I knew it not.

I was young myself in the ministry, and younger in Christian experience. My parochial plans had not as yet assumed such a principle of practical order and inquiry as to make me acquainted with the character and conduct of each family and individual in my flock.

I was then quite a learner, and had much to learn.

And what am I now? A learner still; and if I have learned anything, it is this, that I have every day more and more yet to learn. Of this I am certain, that my young scholar soon became my teacher. I *first* saw what true religion could accomplish in witnessing her experience of it. The Lord once "called a little child unto him, and set him in the midst of his disciples" as an emblem and an illustration of his doctrine. But the Lord did more in the case of little Jane. He not only called *her* as a child to show, by a similitude, what conversion means, but he also called her by his grace to be a vessel of mercy, and a living witness of that almighty power and love by which her own heart was turned to God.

PART II.

There is no illustration of the nature and character of the Redeemer's kingdom on earth which is more grateful to contemplation, than that of the shepherd and his flock. Imagination has been accustomed, from our earliest childhood, to wander amongst the fabled retreats of the Arcadian shepherds. We have probably often delighted ourselves in our own native country, by witnessing the interesting occupation of the pastoral scene. The shepherd, tending his flock on the side of some spacious hill, or in the hollow of a sequestered valley; folding them at night, and guarding them against all danger; leading them from one pasture to another, or for refreshment to the cooling waters. These objects have met and gratified our eyes, as we travelled through the fields, and sought out creation's God, amidst creation's beauties. The poet and the painter have each lent their aid to cherish our delight in these imaginations. Many a descriptive verse has strengthened our attachment to the pastoral scene, and many a well-wrought picture has occasioned it to glow like a reality in our ideas.

But far more impressively than these causes can possibly affect, has the word of God endeared the subject to our hearts, and sanctified it to Christian experience. Who does not look back with love and veneration to those days of holy simplicity, when patriarchs of the church of God lived in tents and watched their flocks? With what a strength and beauty of allusion do the prophets refer to the intercourse between the shepherd and flock for an illustration of the Saviour's kingdom on earth! The Psalmist rejoiced in the consideration that the Lord was his Shepherd, and that therefore he should not want. The Redeemer himself assumed this interesting title, and declared that "his sheep hear his voice, he knows them, and they follow him, and he gives unto them eternal life."

Perhaps at no previous moment was this comparison ever expressed so powerfully, as when his risen Lord gave the pastoral charge to the lately offending but now penitent disciple, saying, "Feed my sheep." Every principle of grace, mercy, and peace, met together on that occasion. Peter had thrice denied his Master: his Master now thrice asked him, "Lovest thou me?" Peter each time appealed to his own, or to his Lord's consciousness of what he felt within his heart. As often Jesus commited to his care the flock which he had purchased with his blood. And that none might be forgotten, he not only said, "Feed my sheep," but "Feed my lambs," also.

May every instructor of the young keep this injunction enforced on his conscience and affections,—I return to little Jane.

It was about fifteen months from the first period of her attendance on my Saturday school, when I missed her from her customary place. Two or three weeks had gone by, without my making any particular inquiry respecting her. I was at length informed that she was not well; but apprehending no peculiar cause for alarm, nearly two months passed away without any further mention of her name being made.

At length a poor old woman in the village, of whose religious disposition I had formed a good opinion, came and said to me, "Sir, have you not missed Jane S— at your house on Saturday afternoons?"

"Yes," I replied, "I believe she is not well."

"Nor ever will be, I fear," said the woman.

"What! do you apprehend any danger in the case?"

"Sir, she is very poorly indeed, and I think is in a decline. She wants to see you, sir; but is afraid you would not come to see such a poor young child as she is."

"Not go where poverty and sickness may call me? How can she imagine so? At which house does she live?"

"Sir, it is a poor place, and she is ashamed to ask you to come there. Her near neighbours are noisy wicked people, and her own father and mother are strange folks. They all make game at poor Jenny because she reads her Bible so much."

"Do not tell me about poor places and wicked people: that is the very situation where a minister of the gospel is called to do the most good. I shall go to see her; you may let her know my intention."

"I will, sir; I go in most days to speak to her, and it does one's heart good to hear her talk."

"Indeed!" said I, "what does she talk about?"

"Talk about, poor thing! why, nothing but good things, such as the Bible, and Jesus Christ, and life, and death, and her soul, and heaven, and hell, and your discourses, and the books you used to teach her, sir. Her father says he'll have no such godly things in his house; and her own mother scoffs at her, and says she supposes Jenny counts herself better than other folks. But she does not mind all that. She will read her books, and then talk so pretty to her mother, and beg that she would think about her soul."

"The Lord forgive me," thought I, "for not being more attentive to this poor child's case!" I seemed to feel the importance of infantine instruction more than ever I had done before, and felt a rising hope that this girl might prove a kind of first-fruits of my labours.

I now recollected her quiet, orderly, diligent attendance on our little weekly meetings; and her marked approbation of the epitaph, as related in my last paper, rushed into my thoughts. "I hope, I really hope," said I, "this dear child will prove a true child of God. And if so, what a mercy to her, and what a mercy for me!"

{Little Jane's Cottage: p137.jpg}

The next morning I went to see the child. Her dwelling was of the humblest kind. It stood against a high bank of earth, which formed a sort of garden behind it. It was so steep, that but little would grow in it; yet that little served to show not only, on the one hand, the poverty of its owners, but also to illustrate the happy truth, that even in the worst of circumstances the Lord does make a kind provision for the support of his creatures. The front aspect of the cottage was chiefly rendered pleasing by a honeysuckle, which luxuriantly climbed up the wall, enclosing the door, windows, and even the chimney, with its twining branches. As I entered the house-door, its flowers put forth a very sweet and refreshing smell. Intent on the object of my visit, I at the same moment offered up silent prayer to God, and entertained a hope, that the welcome fragrance of the shrub might be illustrative of that all-prevailing intercession of a Redeemer, which I trusted was, in the case of this little child, as "a sweet-smelling savour" to her heavenly Father. The very flowers and leaves of the garden and field are emblematical of higher things, when grace teaches us to make them so. Jane was in bed upstairs. I found no one in the house with her except the woman who had brought me the message on the evening before. The instant I looked on the girl, I perceived a very marked change in her countenance: it had acquired the consumptive hue, both white and red. A delicacy unknown to it before quite surprised me, owing to the alteration it produced in her look. She received me first with a very sweet smile, and then instantly burst into a flood of tears, just sobbing out,—

"I am so glad to see you, sir!"

"I am very much concerned at your being so ill, my child, and grieved that I was not sooner aware of your state. But I hope the Lord designs it for your good." Her eye, not her tongue, powerfully expressed, "I hope and think he does."

"Well, my poor child, since you can no longer come to see me, I will come and see you, and we will talk over the subjects which I have been used to explain to you."

"Indeed, sir, I shall be so glad!"

"That I believe she will," said the woman; "for she loves to talk of nothing so much as what she has heard you say in your sermons, and in the books you have given her."

"Are you really desirous, my dear child, to be a true Christian?"

"Oh, yes, yes, sir; I am sure I desire that above all things."

I was astonished and delighted at the earnestness and simplicity with which she spoke these words.

"Sir," added she, "I have been thinking, as I lay on my bed for many weeks past, how good you are to instruct us poor children; what must become of us without it!"

"I am truly glad to perceive that my instructions have not been lost upon you, and pray God that this your present sickness may be an instrument of blessing in his hands to prove, humble, and sanctify you. My dear child, you have a soul, an immortal soul to think of; you remember what I have often said to you about the value of a soul: 'What shall it profit a man, if he gain the whole world, and lose his own soul?'"

"Yes, sir, I remember well you told us, that when our bodies are put into the grave, our souls will then go either to the good or the bad place."

"And to which of these places do you think that, as a sinner in the sight of God, you deserve to go?"

"To the bad one, sir."

"What! to everlasting destruction!"

"Yes, sir."

"Why so?"

"Because I am a great sinner."

"And must all great sinners go to hell?"

"They all deserve it; and I am sure I do."

"But is there no way of escape? Is there no way for a great sinner to be saved?"

"Yes, sir, Christ is the Saviour."

"And whom does he save?"

"All believers."

"And do you believe in Christ yourself?"

"I do not know, sir; I wish I did; but I feel that I love him."

"What do you love him for?"

"Because he is good to poor children's souls like mine."

"What has he done for you?"

"He died for me, sir; and what could he do more?"

"And what do you hope to gain by his death?"

"A good place when I die, if I believe in him, and love him."

"Have you felt any uneasiness on account of your soul?"

"Oh, yes, sir, a great deal. When you used to talk to us children on Saturdays, I often felt as if I could hardly bear it, and wondered that others could seem so careless. I thought I was not fit to die. I thought of all the bad things I had ever done and said, and believed God must be very angry with me; for you often told us, that God would not be mocked; and that Christ said, if we were not converted, we could not go to heaven. Sometimes I thought I was so young it did not signify: and then, again, it seemed to me a great sin to think so; for I knew I was old enough to see what was right and what was wrong; and so God had a just right to be angry when I did wrong. Besides, I could see that my heart was not right; and how could such a heart be fit for heaven? Indeed, sir, I used to feel very uneasy."

"My dear Jenny, I wish I had known all this before. Why did you never tell me about it?"

"Sir, I durst not. Indeed, I could not well say what was the matter with me: and I thought you would look upon me as very bold, if I had spoke about myself to such a gentleman as you: yet I often wished that you knew what I felt and feared. Sometimes, as we went away from your house, I could not help crying; and then the other children laughed and jeered at me, and said I was going to be very good, they supposed, or at least to make people think so. Sometimes, sir, I fancied you did not think so well of me as of the rest, and that hurt me; yet I knew I deserved no particular favour, because I was the chief of sinners."

"My dear, what made St. Paul say he was chief of sinners? In what verse of the Bible do you find this expression, 'the chief of sinners;' can you repeat it?"

"'This is a faithful saying, and worthy of all acceptation, that Christ Jesus came into the world to save sinners;'—is not that right, sir?"

"Yes, my child, it is right; and I hope that the same conviction which St. Paul had at that moment has made you sensible of the same truth. Christ came into the world to save sinners: my dear child, remember now and for ever more, that Christ came into the world to save the chief of sinners."

"Sir, I am so glad he did. It makes me hope that he will save me, though I am a poor sinful girl. Sir, I am very ill, and I do not think I shall ever get well again. I want to go to Christ if I die."

"Go to Christ while you live, my dear child, and he will not cast you away when you die. He that said, 'Suffer little children to come unto me,' waits to be gracious to them, and forbids them not."

"What made you first think so seriously about the state of your soul?"

"Your talking about the graves in the churchyard, and telling us how many young children were buried there. I remember you said, one day, near twelve months ago, 'Children! where will you be a hundred years hence? Children! where do you think you shall go when you die? Children! if you were to die to-night, are you sure you should go to Christ and be happy?' Sir, I never shall forget your saying, 'Children,' three times together in that solemn way."

"Did you ever before that day feel any desire about your soul?"

"Yes, sir; I think I first had that desire almost as soon as you began to teach us on Saturday afternoons; but on that day I felt as I never did before. I shall never forget it. All the way as I went home, and all that night, these words were in my thoughts: 'Children! where do you think you shall go when you die?' I thought I must leave off all my bad ways, or where shall I go when I died?"

"And what effect did these thoughts produce in your mind?"

"Sir, I tried to live better, and I did leave off many bad ways; but the more I strove, the more difficult I found it, my heart seemed so hard: and then I could not tell any one my case."

"Could not you tell it to the Lord, who hears and answers prayers?"

"My prayers (here she blushed and sighed) are very poor at the best, and at that time I scarcely knew how to pray at all as I ought. But I did sometimes ask the Lord for a better heart."

There was a character in all this conversation which marked a truly sincere and enlightened state of mind. She spoke with all the simplicity of a child, and yet the seriousness of a Christian. I could scarcely persuade myself that she was the same girl I had been accustomed to see in past time. Her countenance was filled with interesting affections, and always spoke much more than her tongue could utter. At the same time she now possessed an ease and liberty in speaking, to which she had formerly been a stranger: nevertheless, she was modest, humble, and unassuming. Her readiness to converse was the result of spiritual anxiety, not childish forwardness. The marks of a Divine change were too prominent to be easily mistaken; and in this very child, I, for the first time, witnessed the evident testimonies of such a change. How encouraging, how profitable to my own soul!

"Sir," continued little Jane, "I had one day been thinking that I was neither fit to live nor die: for I could find no comfort in this world, and I was sure I deserved none in the other. On that day you sent me to learn the verse on Mrs. B—'s headstone, and then I read that on the one next to it."

"I very well remember it, Jenny; you came back, and repeated them both to me."

"There were two lines in it which made me think and meditate a great deal."

"Which were they?"

"'Hail Glorious gospel! heavenly light, whereby
We live with comfort, and with comfort die.'

I wished that glorious gospel was mine, that I might live and die with comfort; and it seemed as if I thought it would be so. I never felt so happy in all my life before. The words were often in my thoughts,—

'Live with comfort, and with comfort die.'

Glorious gospel, indeed! I thought."

"My dear child, what is the meaning of the word gospel?"

"Good news."

"Good news for whom?"

"For wicked sinners, sir."

"Who sends this good news for wicked sinners?"

"The Lord Almighty."

"And who brings this good news?"

"Sir, *you* brought it to *me*."

Here my soul melted in an instant, and I could not repress the tears which the emotion excited. The last answer was equally unexpected and affecting. I felt a father's tenderness and gratitude for a new and first-born child.

Jane wept likewise.

After a little pause she said,—

"O sir! I wish you would speak to my father, and mother, and little brother; for I am afraid they are going on very badly."

"How so?"

"Sir, they drink, and swear, and quarrel, and do not like what is good; and it does grieve me so, I cannot bear it. If I speak a word to them about it, they are very angry, and laugh, and bid me be quiet, and not set up for their teacher. Sir, I am ashamed to tell you this of them, but I hope it is not wrong; I mean it for their good."

"I wish your prayers and endeavours for their sake may be blessed; I will also do what I can."

I then prayed with the child, and promised to visit her constantly.

As I returned home, my heart was filled with thankfulness for what I had seen and heard. Little Jane appeared to be a first-fruits of my parochial and spiritual harvest. This thought greatly comforted and strengthened me in my ministerial prospects.

My partiality to the memory of little Jane will probably induce me to lay some further particulars before the reader.

PART III.

Divine grace educates the reasoning faculties of the soul, as well as the best affections of the heart; and happily consecrates them both to the glory of the Redeemer. Neither the disadvantages of poverty, nor the inexperience of childhood, are barriers able to resist the mighty influences of the Spirit of God, when "he goeth forth where he listeth."

"God hath chosen the foolish things of this world to confound the wise; and God hath chosen the weak things of the world to confound the things which are mighty." The truth of this scriptural assertion was peculiarly evident in the case of my young parishioner.

Little Jane's illness was of a lingering nature. I often visited her. The soul of this young Christian was gradually, but effectually, preparing for heaven. I have seldom witnessed in any older person, under similar circumstances, stronger marks of earnest inquiry, continual seriousness, and holy affections. One morning, as I was walking through the church-yard, in my way to visit her, I stopped to look at the epitaph which had made such a deep impression on her mind. I was struck with the reflection of the important consequences which might result from a more frequent and judicious attention to the inscriptions placed in our burying-grounds, as memorials of the departed. The idea occurred to my thoughts, that as the two stone tables given by God to Moses were once a means of communicating to the Jews, from age to age, the revelation of God's will as concerning the law; so these funeral tables of stone may, under a better dispensation, bear a never-failing proclamation of God's will to sinners as revealed in the gospel of his grace, from generation to generation. I have often lamented, when indulging a contemplation among the graves, that some of the inscriptions were coarse and ridiculous; others, absurdly flattering; many, expressive of sentiments at variance with the true principles of the word of God; not a few, barren and unaccompanied with a single word of useful instruction to the reader. Thus a very important opportunity of conveying scriptural admonition is lost. I wish that every grave-stone might not only record the name of our deceased friends, but also proclaim the name of Jesus, as the only name given under heaven whereby men can be saved. Perhaps, if the ministers of religion were to interest themselves in this matter, and accustom their people to consult them as to the nature of the monumental inscriptions which they wish to introduce into churches and church-yards, a gradual improvement would take place in this respect. What is offensive, useless, or erroneous, would no longer find admittance, and a succession of valuable warning and consolation to the living would perpetuate the memory of the dead.

What can be more disgusting than the too common spectacle of trifling licentious travellers, wandering about the church-yards of the different places through which they pass, in search of rude, ungrammatical, ill- spelt, and absurd verses among the grave-stones; and this for the gratification of their unholy scorn and ridicule! And yet how much is it to be deplored that such persons are seldom disappointed in finding many instances which too readily afford them the unfeeling satisfaction which they seek! I therefore offer this suggestion to my reverend brethren, that as no monument or stone can be placed in a church or church-yard without their express consent or approbation, whether one condition of that consent being granted, should not be a previous inspection and approval of every inscription which may be so placed within the precincts of the sanctuary?

The reader will pardon this digression, which evidently arose from the peculiar connection established in little Jane's history, between an epitaph inscribed on a grave-stone, and the word of God inscribed on her heart. When I arrived at Jane's cottage, I found her in bed, reading Dr. Watts' Hymns for Children, in which she took great pleasure.

"What are you reading this morning, Jane?"

"Sir, I have been thinking very much about some verses in my little book. Here they are,—

'There is an hour when I must die,
    Nor do I know how soon 'twill come;
A thousand children young as I
    Are called by death to hear their doom.

Let me improve the hours I have,
    Before the day of grace is fled;
There's no repentance in the grave,
    Nor pardon offered to the dead.'

"Sir, I feel all that to be very true, and I am afraid I do not improve the hours I have, as I ought to do. I think I shall not live very long; and when I remember my sins, I say,—

'Lord, at thy feet ashamed I lie,
    Upward I dare not look;
Pardon my sins before I die,
    And blot them from thy book.'

Do you think he will pardon me, sir?"

"My dear child, I have great hopes that he HAS pardoned you; that he has heard your prayers, and put you into the number of his true children already. You have had strong proofs of his mercy to your soul."

"Yes, sir, I have, and I wish to love and bless him for it. He is good, *very* good."

It had for some time past occurred to my mind that a course of *regulated* conversations on the first principles of religion would be very desirable from time to time, for this interesting child's sake: and I thought the Church Catechism would be the best groundwork for that purpose.

"Jenny," said I, "you can repeat the Catechism?"

"Yes, sir; but I think that has been one of my sins in the sight of God."

"What! repeating your Catechism?"

"Yes, sir, in such a way as I used to do it."

"How was that?"

"Very carelessly indeed. I never thought about the meaning of the words, and that must be very wrong. Sir, the Catechism is full of good things; I wish I understood them better."

"Well, then, my child, we will talk a little about those good things which, as you truly say, are contained in the Catechism. Did you ever consider what it is to be a member of Christ, a child of God, and an inheritor of the kingdom of heaven?"

"I think, sir, I have lately considered it a good deal; and I want to be such, not only in name, but in deed and in truth. You once told me, sir, that 'as the branch is to the vine, and the stone to the building, and the limb to the body and the head, so is a true believer to the Lord Jesus Christ.' But how am I to know that I belong to Christ as a true *member*, which, you said one day in the church, means the same as a *limb* of the body, such as a leg or an arm?"

"Do you love Christ now in a way you never used to do before?"

"Yes, I think so indeed."

"Why do you love him?"

"Because he first loved me."

"How do you know that he first loved you?"

"Because he sent me instruction, and made me feel the sin of my heart, and taught me to pray for pardon, and love his ways; he sent you to teach me, sir, and to show me the way to be saved; and now I want to be saved in that way that he pleases. Sometimes I feel as if I loved all that he has said and done, so much, that I wish never to think about anything else. I know I did not use to feel so; and I think if he had not loved me first, my wicked heart would never have cared about him. I once loved anything better than religion, but now it is everything to me."

"Do you believe in your heart that Christ is able and willing to save the chief of sinners?"

"I do."

"And what are you?"

"A young, but a great sinner."

"Is it not of his mercy that you know and feel yourself to be a sinner?"

"Certainly; yes, it must be so."

"Do you earnestly desire to forsake all sin?"

"If I know myself, I do."

"Do you feel a spirit within you resisting sin, and making you hate it?"

"Yes, I hope so."

"Who gave you that spirit? Were you always so?"

"It must be Christ, who loved me, and gave himself for me. I was quite different once."

"Now, then, my dear Jane, does not all this show a connection between the Lord Jesus Christ and your soul? Does it not seem as if you lived, and moved, and had a spiritual being from him? Just as a limb is connected with your body, and so with your head, and thereby gets power to live and move through the flowing of the blood from the one to the other; so are you spiritually a limb or member of Christ, if you believe in him, and thus obtain, through faith, a power to love him, and live to his praise and glory. Do you understand me?"

"Yes, sir, I believe I do; and it is very comfortable to my thoughts to look up to Christ as a living Head, and to consider myself as the least and lowest of all his members."

"Now tell me what your thoughts are as to being a child of God."

"I am sure, sir, I do not deserve to be called his child."

"Can you tell me who *does* deserve it?"

"No one, sir."

"How, then, comes any one to be a child of God, when by nature we are children of wrath?"

"By God's grace, sir."

"What does grace mean?"

"Favour; free favour to sinners."

"Right; and what does God bestow upon the children of wrath, when he makes them children of grace?"

"A death unto sin, and a new birth unto righteousness; is it not, sir?"

"Yes, this is the fruit of Christ's redeeming love; and I hope *you* are a partaker of the blessing. The family of God is named after him, and he is the first-born of many brethren. What a mercy that Christ calls himself 'a *Brother*!' My little girl, he is *your* Brother; and will not be ashamed to own you, and present you to his Father at the last day, as one that he has purchased with his blood."

"I wish I could love my Father and my Brother which are in heaven better than I do. Lord be merciful to me a sinner! I think, sir, if I am a child of God, I am often a rebellious one. He shows kindness to me beyond others, and yet I make a very poor return.

'Are these thy favours day by day,
    To me above the rest?
Then let me love thee more than they,
    And strive to serve thee best.'"

"That will be the best way to approve yourself a real child of God. Show your love and thankfulness to such a Father, who hath prepared for you an inheritance among the saints in light, and made you 'an inheritor of the kingdom of heaven, as well as a member of Christ, and a child of God.' Do you know what 'the kingdom of heaven' means?"

Just at that instant her mother entered the house below, and began to speak to a younger child in a passionate, scolding tone of voice, accompanied by some very offensive language; but quickly stopped on hearing us in conversation up stairs.

"Ah, my poor mother!" said the girl, "you would not have stopped so short, if Mr. — had not been here. Sir, you hear how my mother swears; pray say something to her; she will not hear me."

I went towards the stair-head, and called to the woman; but ashamed at the thought of my having probably overheard her expressions, she suddenly left the house, and for that time escaped reproof.

"Sir," said little Jane, "I am so afraid, if I go to heaven I shall never see my poor mother there. I wish I may, but she does swear so, and keep such bad company. As I lie here a-bed, sir, for hours together, there is often so much wickedness, and noise, and quarrelling down below, that I do not know how to bear it. It comes very near, sir, when one's father and mother go on so. I want them all to turn to the Lord, and go to heaven.—Tell me now, sir, something about being an inheritor of the kingdom of heaven."

"You may remember, my child, what I have told you when explaining the Catechism in the church, that the 'kingdom of heaven' in the Scripture means the church of Christ upon earth, as well as the state of glory in heaven. The one is a preparation for the other. All true Christians are heirs of God, and joint-heirs with Christ, and shall inherit the glory and happiness of his kingdom, and live with Christ and be with him for ever. This is the free gift of God to his adopted children; and all that believe aright in Christ shall experience the truth of that promise, 'It is your Father's good pleasure to give you the kingdom.' You are a poor girl now, but I trust 'an entrance shall be ministered unto you abundantly into the everlasting kingdom of our Lord and Saviour Jesus Christ.' You suffer now; but are you not willing to suffer for his sake, and to bear patiently those things to which he calls you?"

"Oh yes, very willing; I would not complain. It is all right."

"Then, my dear, you shall reign with him. Through much tribulation you may, perhaps, enter into the kingdom of God; but tribulation worketh patience; and patience, experience; and experience, hope. As a true 'member of Christ,' show yourself to be a dutiful 'child of God,' and your portion will be that of an inheritor of the kingdom of heaven. Faithful is He that hath promised. Commit thy way unto the Lord; trust also in him; and he shall bring it to pass."

"Thank you, sir, I do so love to hear of these things. And I think, sir, I should not love them so much if I had no part in them. Sir, there is one thing I want to ask you. It is a great thing, and I may be wrong—I am so young—and yet I hope I mean right—"

Here she hesitated and paused.

"What is it? Do not be fearful of mentioning it." A tear rolled down her cheek—a slight blush coloured her countenance. She lifted up her eyes to heaven for a moment, and then, fixing them on me with a solemn, affecting look, said,—

"May so young a poor child as I am be admitted to the Lord's Supper? I have for some time wished it, but dared not to mention it, for fear you should think it wrong."

"My dear Jenny, I have no doubt respecting it, and shall be very glad to converse with you on the subject, and hope that He who has given you the desire, will bless his own ordinance to your soul. Would you wish it now or to-morrow?"

"To-morrow, if you please, sir;—will you come to-morrow and talk to me about it? and if you think it proper, I shall be thankful. I am growing faint now—I hope to be better when you come again."

I was much pleased with her proposal, and rejoiced in the prospect of seeing so young and sincere a Christian thus devote herself to the Lord, and receive the sacramental seal of a Saviour's love to her soul.

Disease was making rapid inroads upon her constitution, and she was aware of it. But as the outward man decayed, she was strengthened with might, by God's Spirit in the inner man. She was evidently ripening fast for a better world.

I remember these things with affectionate pleasure; they revive my earlier associations, and I hope the recollection does me good. I wish them to do good to thee likewise, my reader; and therefore I write them down.

May the simplicity that is in Christ render

"The short and simple annals of the poor"

a mean of grace and blessing to thy soul! Out of the mouth of this babe and suckling may God ordain thee strength! If thou art willing, thou mayest perchance hear something further respecting her.

PART IV.

I was so much affected with my last visit to little Jane, and particularly with her tender anxiety respecting the Lord's Supper, that it formed the chief subject of my thoughts for the remainder of the day. I rode in the afternoon to a favourite spot, where I sometimes indulged in solitary meditation; where I wished to reflect on the interesting case of my little disciple.

It was a place well suited for such a purpose.

In the widely sweeping curve of a beautiful bay, there is a kind of chasm or opening in one of the lofty cliffs which bound it. This produces a very romantic and striking effect. The steep descending sides of this opening in the cliff are covered with trees, bushes, wild flowers, fern, wormwood, and many other herbs, here and there contrasted with bold masses of rock or brown earth.

In the higher part of one of those declivities two or three picturesque cottages are fixed, and seem half suspended in the air.

From the upper extremity of this great fissure, or opening in the cliff, a small stream of water enters by a cascade, flows through the bottom, winding in a varied course of about a quarter of a mile in length; and then runs into the sea across a smooth expanse of firm, hard sand, at the lower extremity of the chasm. At this point, the sides of the woody banks are very lofty, and, to a spectator from the bottom, exhibit a mixture of the grand and beautiful not often exceeded.

Near the mouth of this opening was a little hollow recess, or cave in the cliff, from whence, on one hand, I could see the above-described romantic scene; on the other, a long train of perpendicular cliffs, terminating in a bold and wild-shaped promontory, which closed the bay at one end, while a conspicuous white cliff stood directly opposite, about four miles distant, at the further point of the bay.

The shore, between the different cliffs and the edge of the waves, was in some parts covered with stones and shingle; in some, with firm sand; and in others, with irregular heaps of little rocks fringed with sea-weed, and ornamented with small yellow shells.

The cliffs themselves were diversified with strata of various-coloured earth, black, yellow, brown, and orange. The effects of iron ore, producing very manifest changes of hue, were everywhere seen in trickling drops and streamlets down the sides.

The huts in which the fishermen kept their baskets, nets, boats, and other implements, occupied a few retired spots on the shore.

The open sea, in full magnificence, occupied the centre of the prospect; bounded, indeed, in one small part, by a very distant shore, on the rising ascent from which the rays of the sun rendered visible a cathedral church, with its towering spire, at near thirty miles' distance. Everywhere else the sea beyond was limited only by the sky.

A frigate was standing into the bay, not very far from my recess; other vessels of every size, sailing in many directions, varied the scene, and furnished matter for a thousand sources of contemplation.

At my feet the little rivulet, gently rippling over pebbles, soon mingled with the sand, and was lost in the waters of the mighty ocean. The murmuring of the waves, as the tide ebbed or flowed, on the sand; their dashing against some more distant rocks, which were covered fantastically with sea-weed and shells; sea-birds floating in the air aloft, or occasionally screaming from their holes in the cliffs; the hum of human voices in the ships and boats, borne along the water: all these sounds served to promote, rather than interrupt, meditation. They were soothingly blended together, and entered the ear in a kind of natural harmony.

In the quiet enjoyment of a scene like this, the lover of nature's beauties will easily find scope for spiritual illustration.

Here I sat and mused over the interesting character and circumstances of little Jane. Here I prayed that God would effectually teach me those truths which I ought to teach her.

When I thought of her youth, I blushed to think how superior she was to what I well remember myself to have been at the same age; nay, how far my superior at that very time. I earnestly desired to catch something of the spirit which appeared so lovely in her; for, simple, teachable, meek, humble yet earnest in her demeanour, she bore living marks of heavenly teaching.

"The Lord," thought I, "has called this little child, and set her in the midst of us, as a parable, a pattern, an emblem. And he saith, 'Verily, except ye be converted, and become as little children, ye shall not enter into the kingdom of heaven.' Oh that I may be humble as this little child!"

I was thus led into a deep self-examination, and was severely exercised with fear and apprehension, whether I was myself a real partaker of those divine influences which I could so evidently discover in her. Sin appeared to me just then to be more than ever "exceeding sinful." Inward and inbred corruptions made me tremble. The danger of self-deception in so great a matter alarmed me. I was a teacher of others; but was I indeed spiritually taught myself?

A spirit of anxious inquiry ran through every thought: I looked at the manifold works of creation around me; I perceived the greatest marks of regularity and order; but *within* I felt confusion and disorder.

"The waves of the sea," thought I, "ebb and flow in exact obedience to the law of their Creator. Thus far they come, and no further—they retire again to their accustomed bounds; and so maintain a regulated succession of effects.

"But, alas! the waves of passion and affection in the human breast manifest more of the wild confusion of a storm, than the orderly regularity of a tide. Grace only can subdue them.

"What peaceful harmony subsists throughout all this lovely landscape! These majestic cliffs, some clothed with trees and shrubs; others bare and unadorned with herbage, yet variegated with many-coloured earths; these are not only sublime and delightful to behold, but they are answering the end of their creation, and serve as a barrier to stop the progress of the waves.

"But how little peace and harmony can I comparatively see in my own heart! The landscape *within* is marred by dreary, barren wilds, and wants that engaging character which the various parts of this prospect before me so happily preserve. Sin, sin is the bane of mortality, and heaps confusion upon confusion, wherever it prevails.

"Yet, saith the voice of Promise, 'Sin shall not have dominion over you.' Oh, then, 'may I yield myself unto God, as one that am alive from the dead, and my members as instruments of righteousness unto God!' And thus may I become an able and willing minister of the New Testament!

"I wish I were like this little stream of water. It takes its first rise scarcely a mile off; yet it has done good even in that short course. It has passed by several cottages in its way, and afforded life and health to the inhabitants; it has watered their little gardens as it flows, and enriched the meadows near its banks. It has satisfied the thirst of the flocks that are feeding aloft on the hills, and perhaps refreshed the shepherd's boy who sits watching his master's sheep hard by. It then quietly finishes its current in this secluded dell, and, agreeably to the design of its Creator, quickly vanishes in the ocean.

"May *my* course be like unto thine, thou little rivulet! Though short be my span of life, yet may I be useful to my fellow-sinners as I travel onwards! Let me be a dispenser of spiritual support and health to many! Like this stream, may I prove 'the poor man's friend' by the way, and water the souls that thirst for the river of life, wherever I meet them! And if it please thee, O my God, let me in my latter end be like this brook. It calmly, though not quite silently, flows through this scene of peace and loveliness, just before it enters the sea. Let me thus gently close my days likewise; and may I not unusefully tell to others of the goodness and mercy of our Saviour, till I arrive at the vast ocean of eternity!

"Thither," thought I, "little Jane is fast hastening. Short, but not useless, has been *her* course. I feel the great importance of it in my own soul at this moment. I view a work of mercy *there*, to which I do hope I am not quite a stranger in the experience of my own heart. The thought enlivens my spirit, and leads me to see that, great as is the power of sin the power of Jesus is greater; and, through grace, I *may* meet my dear young disciple, my child in the gospel, my sister in the faith, in a brighter, a better world hereafter."

There was something in the whole of this meditation which calmed and prepared my mind for my promised visit the next day. I looked forward to it with affectionate anxiety.

It was now time to return homewards. The sun was setting. The lengthened shadows of the cliffs, and of the hills towering again far above them, cast a brown but not unpleasing tint over the waters of the bay. Further on the beams of the sun still maintained their splendour. Some of the sails of the distant ships, enlivened by its rays, appeared like white spots in the blue horizon, and seemed to attract my notice, as if to claim at least the passing prayer, "God speed the mariners on their voyage."

I quitted my retreat in the cliff with some reluctance; but with a state of mind, as I hoped, solemnized by reflection, and animated to fresh exertion.

I walked up by a steep pathway, that winded through the trees and shrubs on the sides of one of the precipices. At every step the extent of prospect enlarged, and acquired a new and varying character, by being seen through the trees on each side. Climbing up a kind of rude, inartificial set of stone stairs in the bank, I passed by the singularly situated cottages which I had viewed from beneath; received and returned the evening salutation of the inhabitants, sitting at their doors, and just come home from labour; till I arrived at the top of the precipice, where I had left my horse tied to a gate.

Could *he* have enjoyed it, he had a noble prospect around him in every direction from this elevated point of view, where he had been stationed while I was on the shore below. But wherein he most probably failed I think his rider did not. The landscape, taken in connection with my recent train of thought about myself and little Jane, inspired devotion.

The sun was now set: the bright colours of the western clouds, faintly reflected from the south-eastern hills, that were unseen from my retreat in the cliff, or only perceived by their evening shadows on the sea, now added to the beauty of the prospect on the south and west. Every element contributed to the interesting effect of the scenery. The *earth* was diversified in shape and ornament. The *waters* of the ocean presented a noble feature in the landscape. The *air* was serene, or only ruffled by a refreshing breeze from the shore. And the sun's *fiery* beams, though departing for the night, still preserved such a portion of light and warmth as rendered all the rest delightful to an evening traveller. From this point the abyss, occasioned by the great fissure in the cliff, appeared grand and interesting. Trees hung over it on each side, projecting not only their branches, but many of their roots in wild and fantastic forms. Masses of earth had recently fallen from the upper to the lower parts of the precipice, carrying trees and plants down the steep descent. The character of the soil and the unceasing influence of the stream at the bottom, seemed to threaten further slips of the land from the summit. From hence the gentle murmur of the cascade at the head of the chine stole upon the ear without much interruption to the quietness of the scene. A fine rocky cliff, half buried in trees, stood erect on the land side about a mile distant, and seemed to vie with those on the shore in challenging the passenger's attention. In the distance stood a noble ash-tree, which, on a considerable height, majestically reigned as the patriarch of the grove near which it grew. Every object combined to please the eye and direct the traveller's heart to admire and love the Author and Creator of all that is beautiful to sense and edifying to the soul.

The next morning I went to Jane's cottage. On entering the door, the woman, who so frequently visited her, met me, and said:—

"Perhaps, sir, you will not wake her just yet; for she has dropped asleep, and she seldom gets much rest, pool girl!"

I went gently up stairs.

The child was in a half-sitting posture, leaning her head upon her right hand, with her Bible open before her. She had evidently fallen asleep while reading. Her countenance was beautifully composed and tranquil. A few tears had rolled down her cheek, and (probably unknown to her) dropped upon the pages of her book.

I looked around me for a moment. The room was outwardly comfortless and uninviting: the walls out of repair; the sloping roof somewhat shattered; the floor broken and uneven; no furniture but two tottering bedsteads, a three-legged stool, and an old oak chest; the window broken in many places, and mended with patches of paper. A little shelf against the wall, over the bedstead where Jane lay, served for her physic, her food, and her books.

"Yet *here*," I said to myself, "lies an heir of glory, waiting for a happy dismissal. Her earthly home is poor, indeed; but she has a house not made with hands, eternal in the heavens. She has little to attach her to this world; but what a weight of glory in the world to come! This mean, despised chamber is a palace in the eye of faith, for it contains one that is inheritor of a crown."

I approached without waking her, and observed that she had been reading the twenty-third chapter of St. Luke. The finger of her left hand lay upon the book, pointing to the words, as if she had been using it to guide her eye whilst she read.

I looked at the place, and was pleased at the apparently casual circumstance of her finger pointing at these words:—

"Lord, remember me when thou comest into thy kingdom."

"Is this casual or designed?" thought I. "Either way it is remarkable."

But in another moment I discovered that her finger was indeed an index to the thoughts of her heart.

She half awoke from her dozing state, but not sufficiently so to perceive that any person was present, and said in a kind of whisper:—

"Lord, remember me—remember me—remember—remember a poor child—Lord, remember me—"

She then suddenly started and perceived me, as she became fully awake. A faint blush overspread her cheeks for a moment, and then disappeared.

"Dame K—, how long have I been asleep?—Sir, I am very sorry—"

"And I am very glad to find you thus," I replied. "You may say with David, 'I laid me down and slept: I awaked, for the Lord sustained me.' What were you reading?"

"The history of the crucifying of Jesus, sir."

"How far had you read when you fell asleep?"

"To the prayer of the thief that was crucified with him; and when I came to that place I stopped, and thought what a mercy it would be if the Lord Jesus, should remember me likewise—and so I fell asleep; and I fancied in my dream that I saw Christ upon the cross; and I thought I said, 'Lord, remember me;' and I am sure he did not look angry upon me—and then I awoke."

All this seemed to be a sweet commentary on the text, and a most suitable forerunner of our intended sacramental service.

"Well, my dear child, I am come, as you wished me, to administer the sacrament of the body and blood of our blessed Saviour to you; and I daresay neighbour K— will be glad to join us."

"Talk to me a little about it first, sir, if you please."

"You remember what you have learned in your Catechism about it. Let us consider. A sacrament, you know, is 'an outward and visible sign of an inward and spiritual grace, given unto us, ordained by Christ himself, as a means whereby we receive the same, and a pledge to assure us thereof.' Now the Lord has ordained bread and wine in the holy supper, as the outward mark, which we behold with our eyes. It is a sign, a token, a seal of his love, grace, and blessing, which he promises to, and bestows on, all who receive it, rightly believing on his name and work. He in this manner preserves amongst us a 'continual remembrance of his death, and of the benefits which we receive thereby.'"

"What do you believe respecting the death of Christ, Jenny?"

"That because he died, sir, we live."

"What life do we live thereby?"

"The life of grace and mercy *now*, and the life of glory and happiness hereafter; is it not, sir?"

"Yes, assuredly: this is the fruit of the death of Christ, and thus he 'opened the kingdom of heaven to all believers.' As bread and wine strengthen and refresh your poor, weak, fainting body in this very sickness, so does the blessing of his body and blood strengthen and refresh the souls of all that repose their faith, hope, and affections on him who loved us and gave himself for us."

Tears ran down her cheeks as she said,—

"Oh, what a Saviour! Oh, what a sinner! How kind! how good! And is this for me?"

"Fear not, dear child. He that has made you to love him thus, loves you too well to deny you. He will in no wise cast out any that come to him."

"Sir," said the girl, "I can never think about Jesus and his love to sinners, without wondering how it can be. I deserve nothing but his anger on account of my sins. Why then does he love me? My heart is evil. Why then does he love me? I continually forget all his goodness. Why then does he love me? I neither pray to him, nor thank him, nor do anything as I ought to do. Why then such love to me?"

"How plain it is that all is mercy from first to last! and that sweetens the blessing, my child. Are you not willing to give Christ all the honour of your salvation, and to take all the blame of your sins on your own self?"

"Yes, indeed, sir, I am. My hymn says,—

'Blest be the Lord, that sent his Son
    To take our flesh and blood;
He for our lives gave up his own,
    To make our peace with God.

'He honoured all his Father's laws,
    Which we have disobeyed;
He bore our sins upon the cross,
    And our full ransom paid.'"

"I am glad you remember your hymns so well, Jenny."

"Sir, you don't know what pleasure they give me. I am very glad you gave me that little book of Hymns for Children."

A severe fit of coughing interrupted her speech for a while. The woman held her head. It was distressing to observe her struggle for breath, and almost, as it were, for life.

"Poor dear!" said the woman; "I wish I could help thee, and ease thy pains; but they will not last for ever."

"God helps me," said the girl, recovering her breath; "God helps me—he will carry me through. Sir, you look frightened. I am not afraid—this is nothing—I am better now. Thank you, dame, thank you. I am very troublesome; but the Lord will bless you for this and all your kindness to me: yes, sir, and yours too. Now talk to me again about the sacrament."

"What is required, Jenny, of them who come to the Lord's Supper? There are five things named in the Catechism; do you remember what is the first?"

She paused, and then said, with a solemn and intelligent look,—

"To examine themselves whether they repent them truly of their former sins."

"I hope and think that you know what this means, Jenny. The Lord has given you the spirit of repentance."

"No one knows, sir, what the thoughts of past sin have been to me. Yes, the Lord knows, and that is enough; and I hope he forgives me for Christ's sake. His blood cleanseth from all sin. Sir, I sometimes think of my sins till I tremble, and it makes me cry to think that I have offended such a God; and then he comforts me again with sweet thoughts about Christ."

"It is well, my child—be it so. The next thing mentioned in that article of your Catechism, what is it?"

"Steadfastly purposing to lead a new life."

"And what do you think of that?"

"My life, sir, will be a short one; and I wish it had been a better one. But from my heart I desire that it may be a *new* one for the time to come. I want to forsake all my evil ways and thoughts, and evil words, and evil companions; and to do what God bids me, and what you tell me is right, sir, and what I read of in my Bible. But I am afraid I do not, my heart is so full of sin. However, sir, I pray to God to help me. My days will be few; but I wish they may be spent to the glory of God."

"The blessing of the Lord be upon you, Jane; so that whether you live, you may live to the Lord; or whether you die, you may die unto the Lord; and that, living or dying, you may be the Lord's. What is the next thing mentioned?"

"To have a lively faith in God's mercy through Christ, sir."

"Do you believe that God is merciful to you in the pardon of your sins?"

"I do, sir," said the child earnestly.

"And if he pardons you, is it for your own sake, Jenny?"

"No, sir, no; it is for Christ's sake—for my Saviour Jesus Christ's sake, and that only. Christ is all."

"Can you trust him?"

"Sir, I must not mistrust him; nor would I, if I might."

"Right, child; he is worthy of all your trust."

"And then, sir, I am to have a thankful remembrance of his death. I can never think of his dying, but I think also what a poor unworthy creature I am; and yet he is so good to me. I wish I *could* thank him—sir, I have been reading about his death—how could the people do as they did to him?—but it was all for our salvation. And the thief on the cross—that is beautiful. I hope he will remember me too, and that I shall always remember him and his death most thankfully."

"And lastly, Jenny, are you in charity with all men? Do you forgive all that have offended you? Do you bear ill-will in your heart to anybody?"

"Dear sir, no! how can I? If God is good to me, if he forgives me, how can I help forgiving others? There is not a person in all the world, I think, sir, that I do not wish well to for Christ's sake, and that from the bottom of my heart."

"How do you feel towards those bold, wanton, ill-tempered girls at the next door, who jeer and mock you so about your religion?"

"Sir, the worst thing I wish them is, that God may give them grace to repent; that he may change their hearts, and pardon all their wicked ways and words. May he forgive them, as I do with all my soul!"

She ceased—I wished to ask no more. My heart was full. "Can this be the religion of a child?" thought I. "O that we were all children like her!"

"Reach me that prayer-book, and the cup and plate. My dear friends, I will now, with God's blessing, partake with you in the holy communion of our Lord's body and blood."

The time was sweet and solemn. I went through the sacramental service.

The countenance and manner of the child evinced powerful feelings. Tears mingled with smiles—resignation brightened by hope—humility animated by faith—a child-like modesty adorned with the understanding of a riper age—gratitude, peace, devotion, patience—all these were visible. I thought I distinctly saw them all—and did *I* alone see them? Is it too much to say that other created beings, whom I could not behold with my natural eyes, were witnesses of the scene?

If ministering angels do ascend and descend with glad tidings between earth and heaven, I think they did so then.

When I had concluded the service, I said,—

"Now, my dear Jane, you are indeed become a sister in the Church of Christ. May his Spirit and blessing rest upon you, strengthen and refresh you!"

"My mercies are great, very great, sir; greater than I can express. I thank you for this favour—I thought I was too young—it seemed too much for me to think of; but I am now sure the Lord is good to me, and I hope I have done right."

"Yes, Jenny; and I trust you are both outwardly and inwardly *sealed* by the Holy Ghost to the day of redemption."

"Sir, I shall never forget this day."

"Neither, I think, shall I."

"Nor I," said the good old woman; "sure the Lord has been in the midst of us three to-day, while we have been gathered together in his name."

"Sir," said the child, "I wish you could speak to my mother when you come again. But she keeps out of your sight. I am so grieved about her soul, and I am afraid she cares nothing at all about it herself."

"I hope I shall have an opportunity the next time I come. Farewell, my child."

"Good-bye, sir; and I thank you for all your kindness to me."

"Surely," I thought within myself as I left the cottage, "this young bud of grace will bloom beauteously in paradise! The Lord transplant her thither in his own good time. Yet, if it be his will, may she live a little longer, that I may further profit by her conversation and example!"

Possibly, some who peruse these simple records of poor little Jane may wish the same. If it be so, we will visit her again before she departs hence and is no more seen.

PART V.

Jane was hastening fast to her dissolution. She still, however, preserved sufficient strength to converse with much satisfaction to herself and those who visited her. Such as could truly estimate the value of her spiritual state of mind were but few; yet the most careless could not help being struck with her affectionate seriousness, her knowledge of the Scriptures, and her happy application of them to her own case.

"The holy spark divine,"

which regenerating grace had implanted in her life, had kindled a flame which warmed and animated the beholder. To *some*, I am persuaded, her example and conversation were made a blessing. Memory reflects with gratitude, whilst I write, on the profit and consolation which I individually derived from her society. Nor I alone. The last day will, if I err not, disclose further fruits, resulting from the love of God to this little child, and, through her, to others that saw her. And may not hope indulge the prospect, that this simple memorial of her history shall be as one arrow drawn from the quiver of the Almighty to reach the hearts of the young and the thoughtless? Direct its course, O my God! May the eye that reads, and the ear that hears, the record of little Jane, through the power of the Spirit of the Most High, each become the witness for the truth as it is in Jesus!

I remembered the tender solicitude of this dear child for her mother. I well knew what an awful contrast the dispositions and conduct of her parents exhibited, when compared with her own.

I resolved to avail myself of the first opportunity I could seize to speak to the mother in the child's presence. The woman had latterly avoided me, conscious of deserving, and fearful of receiving reproof. The road by which I usually approached the house lay, for some little distance, sufficiently in sight of its windows to enable the woman to retire out of the way before I arrived. There was, however, another path, through fields at the back of the village, which, owing to the situation of the ground, allowed of an approach unperceived, till a visitor reached the very cottage itself.

One morning, soon after the sacramental interview related in my last paper, I chose *this* road for my visit. It was preferable to me on every account. The distance was not quite half a mile from my house. The path was retired. I hereby avoided the noise and interruption which even a village street will sometimes present, to disturb the calmness of interesting meditation.

As I passed through the churchyard, and cast my eye on the memorable epitaph, "Soon," I thought within me, "will my poor little Jane mingle her mouldering remains with this dust, and sleep with her fathers! Soon will the youthful tongue, which now lisps hosannas to the Son of David, and delights my heart with evidences of early piety and grace, be silent in the earth! Soon shall I be called to commit her 'body to the ground, earth to earth, ashes to ashes, dust to dust.' But oh, what a glorious change! Her spirit shall have then returned to God who gave it. Her soul will be joining the halleluiahs of paradise, while we sing her requiem at the grave. And her very dust shall here wait, in sure and certain hope of a joyful resurrection from the dead."

I went through the fields without meeting a single individual. I enjoyed the retirement of my solitary walk. Various surrounding objects contributed to excite useful meditation connected with the great subjects of time and eternity. Here and there a drooping flower reminded me of the fleeting nature of mortal life. Sometimes a shady spot taught me to look to Him who is a "shadow in the day-time from the heat, and for a place of refuge, and for a covert from storm and from rain." If a worm crept across my path, I saw an emblem of myself as I am *now*; and the winged insects, fluttering in the sunbeams, led me comparatively to reflect on what I hoped to be *hereafter*.

The capacious mansion of a rich neighbour appeared on the right hand as I walked; on my left were the cottages of the poor. The church spire pointing to heaven a little beyond, seemed to say to both the rich and the poor, "Set your affection on things above, not on things on the earth." All these objects afforded me useful meditation; and all obtained an increased value as such, because they lay in my road to the house of little Jane.

I was now arrived at the stile nearly adjoining her dwelling. The upper window was open, and I soon distinguished the sound of voices—I was glad to hear that of the mother. I entered the house door unperceived by those above stairs, and sat down below, not wishing as yet to interrupt a conversation which quickly caught my ear.

"Mother! mother! I have not long to live. My time will be very short. But I must, indeed I must, say something for your sake, before I die. O mother! you have a soul—you have a soul; and what will become of it when you die? O my mother! I am so uneasy about your soul—"

"Oh, dear! I shall lose my child—she will die—and what shall I do when you are gone, my Jenny?" She sobbed aloud.

"Mother, think about your soul. Have you not neglected that?"

"Yes, I have been a wicked creature, and hated all that was good. What can I do?"

"Mother, you must pray to God to pardon you for Christ's sake. You must pray."

"Jenny, my child, I cannot pray: I never did pray in all my life. I am too wicked to pray."

"Mother, I have been wanting to speak to you a long time; but I was afraid to do it. You did not like me to say anything about religion, and I did not know how to begin. But indeed, mother, I must speak now, or it may be too late. I wish Mr. — was here, for he could talk to you better than I can. But perhaps you will think of what I say, poor as it is, when I am dead. I am but a young child, and not fit to speak about such things to anybody. But, mother, you belong to me, and I cannot bear to think of your perishing for ever. My Lord and Saviour has shown me my own sin and corruptions: he loved me, and gave himself for me: he died, and he rose again: I want to praise him for it for ever and ever. I hope I shall see him in heaven; but I want to see you there too, mother. Do, pray do, leave off swearing, and other bad ways: go to church, and hear our minister speak about Jesus Christ, and what he has done for wicked sinners. He wishes well to souls. He taught me the way, and he will teach you, mother. Why did you always go out of the house when he was coming? Do not be angry with me, mother; I only speak for your good. I was once as careless as you are about the things of God. But I have seen my error. I was in the broad road leading to destruction, like many other children in the parish; and the Lord saw me, and had mercy upon me."

"Yes, my child, you were always a good girl, and minded your book."

"No, mother, no; not always. I cared nothing about goodness, nor my Bible, till the minister came and sent for us, as you know, on Saturday afternoons. Don't you remember, mother, that at first you did not like me to go, and said you would have no such *godly*, *pious* doings about *your* house; and that I had better play about the streets and fields, than be laughed at and be made game of for pretending to be so good? Ah, mother, you did not know what I went for, and what God designed for me and my poor sinful soul! But, thank God, I did go, and there learned the way of salvation. Mother, I wish you had learned too."

As I listened to this affecting conversation, it appeared to me, from the tone and manner of the mother's voice, that she was more under the influence of temporary grief, on account of her child's extreme illness, than sincere sorrow from any real sense of her sins. I however hoped the best, and rejoiced to hear such weighty and important exhortation dropping from her daughter's lips. I felt that present circumstances rendered it far more valuable than my own could have been.

I have often, since that time, seen the wicked and careless much affected, while sitting by the dying bed of a near relative: I have witnessed their temporary acknowledgments of sin, and heard their professions of amendment. But, after a short season, all has passed away like the morning dew. The friend has been buried out of sight. The world and its cares, the flesh and its sins, have returned with new temptations, and the eloquence of iniquity has prevailed over the voice of truth. "The dog has returned to his vomit, and the sow to her wallowing in the mire."

On the other hand, how frequently have the deathbeds of true believers been blessed to the eye-witness of the triumphs of grace over sin, death, and hell! Often has the careless bystander received the first saving impression of divine truth, whilst the dying Christian has experienced and testified the supports of love and mercy in the trying hour. At such seasons, faith wields a bright and burning torch, which occasionally softens the hardest and warms the coldest heart. The expressions of that heavenly consolation and devout solicitude, which the Holy Spirit vouchsafes to some, thus become the happy means of grace and blessing for the conversion and edification of others.

"He that hath an ear, let him hear what the Spirit saith unto the churches!"

At this moment the house-door opened, and a younger child, a brother of Jane's, came in. The mother asked from above who it was: the boy replied; and, without further inquiry, she remained in the chamber. I beckoned to the lad to sit down quietly; and thus it still remained unknown that I was below.

"Mother," continued Jane, "that is my brother, and will soon be your only remaining child. Do, pray, encourage him to follow good ways. Send him to Mr. —, and he will be kind to him, as he has been to me. He is a wild boy, but I hope he will be brought to think about his soul in time. Those naughty, wicked boys teach him to swear and fight, and run after all manner of evil. Lord, help him to flee from the wrath to come!"

I made a sign to the boy to listen to what his sister said concerning him. He seemed to hear with attention, and a tear dropped down his cheek.

"Ay, Jenny, it is to be hoped he will, and that we shall all likewise."

"Mother, then you must flee to Christ. Nothing you can do will save you without that. You must repent and turn from sin: without the grace of God you cannot do it; but seek, and you shall find it. Do, for your own sake, and for my sake, and my little brother's sake."

The woman wept and sobbed without replying. I now thought it time to appear, went to the bottom of the stairs, and said, "May a friend come up?"

"Mercy on me!" said the mother, "there is Mr. —"

"Come in, sir," said Jane; "I am very glad you are come *now*. Mother, set a chair."

The woman looked confused. Jane smiled as I entered, and welcomed me as usual.

"I hope I shall be forgiven, both by mother and daughter, for having remained so long below stairs, during the conversation which has just taken place. I came in the hope of finding you together, as I have had a wish for some time past to speak to you, Sarah, on the same subjects about which, I am happy to say, your daughter is so anxious. You have long neglected these things, and I wished to warn you of the danger of your state; but Jenny has said all I could desire, and I now solemnly ask you, whether you are not much affected by your poor child's faithful conversation? You ought to have been *her* teacher and instructor in the ways of righteousness, whereas she has now become *yours*. Happy, however, will it be for you if you are wise, and consider your latter end, and the things which belong to your peace, before they are hidden from your eyes! Look at your dying child, and think of your other and only remaining one, and say whether this sight does not call aloud upon you to hear and fear."

Jane's eyes were filled with tears whilst I spoke. The woman hung her head down, but betrayed some emotions of dislike at the plain dealing used towards her.

"My child, Jenny," said I, "how are you to-day?"

"Sir, I have been talking a good deal, and feel rather faint and weary, but my mind has been very easy and happy since I last saw you. I am quite willing to die, when the Lord sees fit. I have no wish to live except it be to see my friends in a better way before I depart. Sir, I used to be afraid to speak to them; but I feel to-day as if I could hold my peace no longer, and I must tell them what the Lord has done for my soul, and what I feel for theirs."

There was a firmness, I may say a dignity with which this was uttered that surprised me. The character of the child seemed to be lost in that of the Christian; her natural timidity yielded to a holy assurance of manner resulting from her own inward consolations, mingled with spiritual desire for her mother's welfare. This produced a flush upon her otherwise pallid countenance, which in no small degree added to her interesting appearance. The Bible lay open before her as she sat up in the bed. With her right hand she enclosed her mother's.

"Mother, this book *you* cannot read; you should therefore go constantly to church, that you may hear it explained. It is God's book, and tells us the way to heaven; I hope you will learn and mind it; with God's blessing it may save your soul. Do think of that, mother, pray do. I am soon going to die. Give this Bible to my brother; and will you be so kind, sir, as to instruct him? Mother, remember what I say, and this gentleman is witness: there is no salvation for sinners like you and me but in the blood of Christ; he is able to save to the uttermost; he will save all that come to him; he waits to be gracious: cast yourself upon his mercy. I wish—I wish—I—I—I—"

She was quite overcome, and sank away in a kind of fainting fit.

Her mother observed, that she would now probably remain insensible for some time before she recovered.

I improved this interval in a serious address to the woman, and then prepared to take my departure, perceiving that Jane was too much exhausted for further conversation at that time.

As I was leaving the room, the child said faintly, "Come again soon, sir; my time is very short."

I returned home by the same retired road which I had before chosen. I silently meditated on the eminent proofs of piety and faith which were just afforded me in the scene I had witnessed.

Surely, I thought, this is an extraordinary child! What cannot grace accomplish? Is it possible to doubt after this, *who* is the alone Author and Finisher of salvation; or from *whom* cometh every good and perfect gift? How rich and free is the mercy of Jehovah! Hath not he "chosen the weak things of this world to confound the things which are mighty?" Let no flesh glory in his presence: but "he that glorieth, let him glory in the Lord."

PART VI.

The truth and excellence of the religion of Jesus Christ appear to be remarkably established by the union of similarity with variety, in the effect which it produces on the hearts and lives of true believers. In the grand and essential features of Christian experience, the whole household of God possess an universal sameness of character, a family likeness, which distinguishes them from all the world besides: yet, in numerous particulars, there also exists a beautiful variety.

On the one hand, in the aged and the young, in the wise and the unlearned, in the rich and the poor; in those of stronger and weaker degrees of mental capacity, in more sanguine or more sedate dispositions; and in a multitude of otherwise varying circumstances, there is a striking conformity of principles and feeling to Christ, and to each other. Like the flowers of the field and the garden, they are "all rooted and grounded" in the soil of the same earth; they are warmed by the same sun, refreshed by the same air, and watered by the same dews. They each derive nourishment, growth, and increase from the same life- giving Source. As the flower puts forth its leaves and petals, adorns the place which it inhabits with its beauty, and possesses an internal system of qualities, whereby it is enabled to bring forth its seed or fruit in the appointed season; so does the Christian.

But, on the other hand, like the flowers also, some Christians may be said to grow on the mountain tops, some in valleys, some in the waters, and others in dry ground. Different colours, forms, and sizes, distinguish them from each other, and produce a diversity of character and appearance which affords a delightful variety, both for the purposes of use and beauty. Yet is that variety perfectly consistent with their essential unity of nature in the vegetable kingdom, to which they all equally belong.

In another particular they likewise resemble. They both die a natural death. The Lord ever preserves "a seed to serve him," from generation to generation; for as one disappears, another springs up to supply his place. But "it is appointed unto all men once to die."—Man "cometh forth like a flower and is cut down: he fleeth also as a shadow, and continueth not."—"All flesh is as grass, and all the glory of man as the flower of the grass. The grass withereth, and the flower thereof falleth away."

In the midst of such diversity of Christian characters there is much to love and admire. I have selected the case of little Jane, as one not undeserving of notice.

It is true, she was only a child—a very poor child—but a child saved by divine grace, enlightened with the purest knowledge, and adorned with unaffected holiness; she was a child, humble, meek, and lowly. She "found grace in the eyes of the Lord" while she was on earth; and, I doubt not, will be seen on his right hand at the last day. As such, there is preciousness in the character, which will account for my attempting once more to write concerning her, and describe her last moments before she went to her final rest.

At a very early hour on the morning of the following day, I was awoke by the arrival of a messenger, bringing an earnest request that I would immediately go to the child, as her end appeared to be just approaching.

It was not yet day when I left my house to obey the summons. The morning star shone conspicuously clear. The moon cast a mild light over the prospect, but gradually diminished in brightness as the eastern sky became enlightened. The birds were beginning their songs, and seemed ready to welcome the sun's approach. The dew plentifully covered the fields, and hung suspended in drops from the trees and hedges. A few early labourers appeared in the lanes, travelling towards the scene of their daily occupations.

All besides was still and calm. My mind, as I proceeded, was deeply exercised by thoughts concerning the affecting event which I expected soon to witness.

The rays of the morning star were not so beautiful in my sight, as the spiritual lustre of this young Christian's character. "Her night was far spent;" the morning of a "better day was at hand." The sun of eternal blessedness was ready to break upon her soul with rising glory. Like the moon, which I saw above me, this child's exemplary deportment had gently cast a useful light over the neighbourhood where she dwelt. Like this moon she had for a season been permitted to shine amidst the surrounding darkness; and her rays were also reflected from a luminary, in whose native splendour her own would quickly be blended and lost.

The air was cool, but the breezes of the morning were refreshing, and seemed to foretell the approach of a beautiful day. Being accustomed, in my walks, to look for subjects of improving thought and association, I found them in every direction around me as I hastened onwards to the house where Jane lay, waiting for a dismissal from her earthly dwelling.

I felt that the twilight gravity of nature was, at that hour, peculiarly appropriate to the circumstances of the case; and the more so, because that twilight was significantly adorned with the brilliant sparklings of the star on one hand, and the clear, pale lustre of the waning moon on the other.

When I arrived at the house, I found no one below; I paused for a few minutes, and heard the girl's voice very faintly saying, "Do you think he will come? I should be so glad—so very glad to see him before I die."

I ascended the stairs—her father, mother, and brother, together with the elderly woman before spoken of, were in the chamber. Jane's countenance bore the marks of speedy dissolution. Yet, although death was manifest in the languid features, there was something more than ever interesting in the whole of her external aspect. The moment she saw me, a renewed vigour beamed in her eye; grateful affection sparkled in the dying face.

Although she had spoken just before I entered, yet for some time afterwards she was silent, but never took her eyes off me. There was animation in her look—there was more—something like a foretaste of heaven seemed to be felt, and gave an inexpressible character of spiritual beauty, even in death.

At length she said, "This is very kind, sir—I am going fast—I was afraid I should never see you again in this world."

I said, "My child, are you resigned to die?"

"Quite."

"Where is your hope?"

She lifted up her finger, pointed to heaven, and then directed the same downward to her own heart, saying successively as she did so, "Christ *there*, and Christ *here*."

These words, accompanied by the action, spoke her meaning more solemnly than can easily be conceived.

A momentary spasm took place. Looking towards her weeping mother, she said, "I am very cold—but it is no matter—it will soon be over—"

She closed her eyes for about a minute, and, on opening them again, said, "I wish, sir, when I am gone, you would tell the other children of the parish how good the Lord has been to me, a poor sinner—tell them, that they who seek him early will find him—tell them, that the ways of sin and ignorance are the ways to ruin and hell—and pray tell them, sir, from me, that Christ is indeed the Way, the Truth, and the Life—he will in no wise cast out any that come. Tell them that I, a poor girl—"

She was quite exhausted, and sunk for a while into a torpid state, from which, however, she recovered gradually, uttering these expressions: "Where am I?—I thought I was going—Lord, save me!"

"My dear child, you will soon be for ever in *His* arms who is now guiding you by his rod and staff through the valley of the shadow of death."

"I believe so, indeed I do," said she; "I long to be with him!—Oh, how good, how great, how merciful!—Jesus, save me, help me through this last trial!"

She then gave one hand to her father, the other to her mother, and said, "God bless you, God bless you—seek the Lord—think of me when I am gone—it may be for your good—remember your souls—oh, for Christ's sake remember your souls—then all may be well—you cannot know what I have felt for both of you—Lord, pardon and save my dear father and mother!"

She then took hold of her brother's hand, saying, "Thomas, I beg you to leave off your bad ways—read the Bible—I give you mine—I have found it a precious book. Do you not remember our little brother, who died some years since?—he was praying to the last moment of his life. Learn to pray while you are in health, and you will find the comfort and power of it when you come to die; but, first of all, pray for a new heart—without it you will never see God in heaven—your present ways lead to misery and ruin—may the Lord turn your heart to love and follow him!"

To the other woman she said, "I thank you, Dame K——, for all your kindness since I have been ill—you have been a Christian friend to me, and I hope that the Lord will remember you for it, according to his rich mercy:—you and I have many a time talked together about death; and though I am the youngest, he calls me first to pass through it: but, blessed be his name, I am not terrified. I once thought I could never die without fear; but indeed I feel quite happy, now it is come; and so will you, if you trust him—he is the God both of the old and the young."

"Ah, my child!" said the woman, "I wish I was as fit to die as you are; but I fear that will never be—my sins have been many, very many."

"Christ's blood cleanseth from all sin," said the child.

At this moment, instead of growing weaker, through the fatigue of so much speaking, she seemed to gather fresh strength. She turned to me with a look of surprising earnestness and animation, saying,—

"You, sir, have been my best friend on earth—you have taught me the way to heaven, and I love and thank you for it—you have borne with my weakness and my ignorance—you have spoken to me of the love of Christ, and he has made me to feel it in my heart—I shall see him face to face—he will never leave me nor forsake me—he is the same, and changes not. Dear sir, God bless you!"

The child suddenly rose up, with an unexpected exertion, threw her livid, wasted arms around me, as I sat on the bedside, laid her head on my shoulder, and said distinctly, "God bless and reward you—give thanks for me to him—my soul is saved—Christ is everything to me! Sir, we shall meet in heaven, shall we not?—Oh yes, yes—then all will be peace—peace—peace—"

She sank back on the bed, and spoke no more—fetched a deep sigh—smiled—and died.

At this affecting moment, the rays of the morning sun darted into the room, and filled my imagination with the significant emblem of "the tender mercy of our God; whereby the dayspring from on high hath visited us, to give light to them that sit in darkness and in the shadow of death, to guide our feet into the way of peace."

It was a beam of light that seemed at once to describe the glorious change which her soul had now already experienced; and, at the same time, to shed the promised consolations of hope over the minds of those who witnessed her departure.

This was an incident obviously arising from a natural cause; but one which irresistibly connected itself with the spiritual circumstances of the case.

For some time I remained silently gazing on the breathless corpse, and could hardly persuade myself that Jane was indeed no longer there.

As I returned homeward, I found it difficult to repress the strong feelings of affection which such a scene had excited. Neither did I wish it. Religion, reason, and experience, rather bid us indulge, in due place and season, those tender emotions, which keep the heart alive to its most valuable sensibilities. To check them serves but to harden the mind, and close the avenues which lead to the sources of our best principles of action.

Jesus himself *wept* over the foreseen sorrows of Jerusalem. He *wept* also at the grave of his friend Lazarus. Such an example consecrates the tear of affection, while it teaches us, concerning them which are asleep, not to sorrow, as those which have no hope.

I soon fell into meditation on the mysterious subject of the flight of a soul from this world to that of departed spirits.

"Swifter than an arrow from the bow, or than the rays of light from the sun, has this child's spirit hastened, in obedience to its summons from God, to appear in his immediate presence. How solemn a truth is this for universal consideration! But, 'washed in the blood of the Lamb that was slain,' and happily made partaker of its purifying efficacy, she meets her welcome at the throne of God. She has nothing to fear from the frowns of divine justice. Sin, death, and hell, are all vanquished through the power of Him who hath made her more than conqueror. He will himself present her to his Father, as one of the purchased lambs of his flock—as one whom the Spirit of God 'has sealed unto the day of redemption.'

"What a change for her!—from that poor tattered chamber to the regions of paradise!—from a bed of straw to the bosom of Abraham!—from poverty, sickness, and pain, to eternal riches, health, and joy!—from the condition of a decayed, weary pilgrim in this valley of tears, to that of a happy traveller safely arrived at home, in the rest that remaineth to the people of God!

"I have lost a young disciple, endeared to me by a truly parental tie. Yet how can I complain of that as lost which God has found? Her willing and welcome voice no longer seeks or imparts instruction here. But it is far better employed. The angels, who rejoiced over her when her soul first turned to God, who watched the progress of her short pilgrimage, and who have now carried her triumphantly to the heavenly hills, have already taught her to join

'In holy song, their own immortal strains.'

Why then should I mourn? The whole prospect, as it concerns her, is filled with joy and immortality: 'Death is swallowed up in victory.'"

As I looked upon the dewdrops which rested on the grass and hung from the branches of the trees, I observed that the sun's rays first filled them with beautiful and varied colours; then dried them up, and they were seen no longer.

Thus it was with myself. The tears which I neither would nor could restrain, when I first began thus to reflect on the image of the dying chamber of little Jane, were speedily brightened by the vivid sunshine of hope and confidence. They then gradually yielded to the influence of that divine principle which shall finally wipe the tear from every eye, and banish all sorrow and sighing for evermore.

On the fourth day from thence, Jane was buried. I had never before committed a parishioner to the ground with similar affections. The attendants were not many, but I was glad to perceive among them some of the children who had been accustomed to receive my weekly private instruction along with her.

I wished that the scene might usefully impress their young hearts, and that God would bless it to their edification.

As I stood at the head of the grave, during the service, I connected past events, which had occurred in the churchyard, with the present. In this spot Jane first learned the value of that gospel which saved her soul. Not many yards from her own burial-place, was the epitaph which has already been described as the first means of affecting her mind with serious and solemn conviction. It seemed to stand at *this* moment as a peculiar witness for those truths which its lines proclaimed to every passing reader. Such an association of objects produced a powerful effect on my thoughts.

The evening was serene—nothing occurred to interrupt the quiet solemnity of the occasion.

"Peace" was the last word little Jane uttered while living; and peace seemed to be inscribed on the farewell scene of the grave where she was laid. A grateful remembrance of that peace revives in my own mind, as I write these memorials of it; and oh, may that peace which passeth all understanding be in its most perfect exercise, when I shall meet her again at the last day!

Attachment to the spot where this young Christian lay, induced me to plant a yew-tree close by the head of her grave, adjoining the eastern wall of the church. I designed it as an evergreen monument of one who was dear to memory. The young plant appeared healthy for a while, and promised by its outward vigour long to retain its station. But it withered soon afterwards, and, like the child whose grave it pointed out to notice, early faded away and died.

The yew-tree proved a frail and short-lived monument. But a more lasting one dwells in my own heart. And perhaps this narrative may be permitted to transmit her memory to other generations, when the hand and heart of the writer shall be cold in the dust.

Perchance some, into whose hands these pages may fall, will be led to cultivate their spiritual young plants with increased hopes of success, in so arduous an endeavour. May the tender blossoms reward their care, and bring forth early and acceptable fruit!

Some, who have perhaps been accustomed to undervalue the character of *very* youthful religion, may hereby see that the Lord of grace and glory is not limited in the exercise of his power by age or circumstance. It sometimes appears in the displays of God's love to sinners, as it does in the manifestations of his works in the heavens, that the *least* of the planets moves in the nearest course to the sun; and there enjoys the most powerful influence of his light, heat, and attraction.

The story of this Young Cottager involves a clear evidence of the freeness of the operations of divine grace on the heart of man; of the inseparable connection between true faith and holiness of disposition; and of the simplicity of character which a real love of Christ transfuses into the soul.

How many of the household of faith of every age,

"Alike unknown to fortune and to fame,"

have journeyed and are now travelling to their "city of habitation," through the paths of modest obscurity and almost unheeded piety! It is one of the most interesting employments of the Christian minister to search out these spiritual lilies of the valley, whose beauty and fragrance are nearly concealed in their shady retreats. To rear the flower, to assist in unfolding its excellences, and bring forth its fruit in due season, is a work that delightfully recompenses the toil of the cultivator.

While he is occupied in this grateful task of labouring in his heavenly Master's garden, some blight, some tempest, may chance to take away a favourite young blossom in a premature stage of its growth.

If such a case should befall him, he will then, perhaps, as I have often done, when standing in pensive recollection at little Jane's grave, make an application of these lines, which are inscribed on a grave-stone erected in the same churchyard, and say—

"This lovely bud so young and fair,
    Called hence by early doom,
Just came to show how sweet a flower
    In paradise would bloom."

THE COTTAGE CONVERSATION

As I journeyed late on a summer evening, meditating on the beauties of the prospect around me, while they gradually faded from my sight, through the approach of darkness, it grew suddenly quite gloomy, and a black cloud hanging over my head threatened a heavy shower of rain. The big drops began to fall, and an open shed, adjoining to a labourer's cottage, offering me a seasonable shelter, I dismounted from my horse, and found it large enough to protect him as well as myself.

The circumstance reminded me of the happy privilege of the believing sinner, who finds a "refuge from the storm, and the blast of the terrible ones, in the love of his Redeemer," which prepares him "a covert from storm and from rain." I went in unperceived: the door of the cottage was half open, and I heard the voices of a poor man, his wife, and some children within.

I was hesitating whether to go into the house and make myself known, or to enjoy in solitude a meditation on the foregoing comparison, which my situation had brought to my mind, when these words, spoken in a calm and affectionate tone, struck me with mingled pleasure and surprise, and determined me not to interrupt the conversation:—

"Indeed, wife, you are in the wrong. Riches would never make us happier, so long as the Lord sees it good that we should be poor."

"Well," replied the wife, "I can see no harm in wishing for more money and better living than we have at present. Other people have risen in the world; and why should not we? There's neighbour Sharp has done well for his family, and, for anything I can see, will be one of the richest farmers in the parish, if he lives; and everybody knows he was once as poor as we are: while you and I are labouring and toiling from morning to night, and can but just get enough to fill our children's mouths, and keep ourselves coarsely clothed, and hardly that."

"Wife," answered the man, "having food and raiment, let us therewith be content. And if it please God that even these things should fall short, let us submit ourselves to God in patience and well-doing, for he gives us more than we deserve."

"There, now you are got to preaching again," said the woman; "you never give me an answer, but you must always go to your Bible to help you out."

"And where can I go so well?" replied the husband. "Is it not God's own word for our instruction?"

"Well, that may be, but I don't like so much of it," answered she.

"And I do not like so little of it as I see and hear from you," returned the man.

"Why, that book has taught me that it is an honour and comfort to be a poor man, and, by the blessing of the Spirit of God, I believe and feel it to be true. I have, through mercy, always been enabled to get the bread of honest industry, and so have you; and though our children feed upon brown bread, and we cannot afford to buy them fine clothes, like some of our vain neighbours, to pamper their pride with; yet, bless the Lord, they are as healthy and clean as any in the parish. Why then should you complain? Godliness with contentment is great gain!"

"An honour and a comfort to be a poor man, indeed! What nonsense you talk! What sort of honour and comfort can that be? I am out of patience with you, man," the wife sharply cried out.

"I can prove it!" replied he.

"How?" returned his partner, in no very pleasant tone of voice.

"My dear," said the good man, "hear me quietly, and I will tell you."

"I think it an honour, and I feel it a comfort, to be in that very station of life which my Saviour Jesus Christ was in before me. He did not come into the world as one that was rich and great, but as a poor man, who had not where to lay his head. I feel a blessing in my poverty, because Jesus, like me, was poor. Had I been a rich man, perhaps I should never have known nor loved him. 'For not many mighty, not many noble, are called.' God's people are chiefly found among the base things of the world, and things which are despised. This makes my poverty to be my comfort.

"Besides, hath not God chosen the poor of this world, rich in faith, and heirs of the kingdom which he hath promised to them that love him? This thought makes my poverty also to be my honour.

"Moreover, to the poor the gospel was and is preached, and to my heart's delight I find it to be true, every Sunday of my life. And is it not plain, all the neighbourhood through, that while so many of our rich farmers, and tradesmen, and squires, are quite careless, or set their faces against the ways of God, and are dead to everything that is gracious and holy; a great number of the poorest people are converted and live? I honour the rich for their station, but I do not envy them for their possessions. I can not forget what Christ once said, 'How hardly shall they that have riches enter into the kingdom of God!'

"Oh! my dear wife, if you did but know how to set a right value upon the precious promises which God has made to the poor, how thankful should I be!

"The expectation of the poor shall not perish. He delivereth the poor and needy from him that spoileth him. He has prepared of his goodness for the poor. The poor among men shall rejoice in the holy one. For he became poor, that we, through his poverty might be rich; not in gold, but in grace.

"These promises comfort my soul, and would make me happy, even if I were deprived of that which I now enjoy. I can trust my Saviour for this world as well as for the next. He that spared not his own Son, but delivered him up for us all, how shall he not with him also freely give us all things?

"The Lord of his mercy bless you, my dear Sarah, with the grace of a contented mind!"

Here the gracious man stopped: and whether affected by her husband's discourse, or by any other cause, I know not, but she made no reply. He then said, "Come, children, it is our time for rest; shut the door, and let us go to prayer."

"Forgive me," said I, laying hold of the door, as the child was obeying her father's orders, "if I ask leave to make one in your family devotions, before I travel homeward. I have heard you, my friend, when you knew it not, and bless God for the sermon which you have this night preached to my heart."

The honest labourer blushed for a moment at this unexpected intrusion and declaration, but immediately said, "Sir, you are welcome to a poor man's dwelling, if you come in the name of the Lord."

I just looked round at the wife, who seemed to be startled at my sudden appearance, and the six fine children who sat near her, and then said, "You were going to pray; I must beg of you, without regarding me, to go on as if I were not here."

The man, whom I could not but love and reverence, with a simple, unaffected, modest, and devout demeanour, did as I requested him. His prayer was full of tender affection and sincerity, expressed with great Scriptural propriety, and was in all respects such as became the preacher of those sentiments which I have overheard him deliver to his wife just before.

When he had finished, each of his children, according to the good old patriarchal custom of better days, kneeled down before him in turn to receive a father's blessing.

It was now late, and the rain was over. I gave the poor man my blessing, and received his in return. I wished them good night, and went onwards to my own home, reflecting with much self-abasement of heart, what an honour and comfort it is to be a poor man, rich in faith.

A VISIT TO THE INFIRMARY.

I went a few months since to visit a parishioner, then in the county infirmary, within some miles of which I reside, and was informed that in an adjoining ward there lay a very good old man, confined by a mortification in his foot, who would take particular satisfaction in any Christian conversation which my time would allow me to afford him.

The nurse conducted me into a room where I found him alone on a bed. The character of his countenance was venerable, cheerful, contented, and pious. His hoary hairs proclaimed him to be aged, although the liveliness in his eye was equal to that of the most vigorous youth.

"How are you, my friend?" I said.

"Very well, sir, very well. Never better in all my life. Thank God for all his mercies!" replied the man, with so cheerful a tone of voice as at once surprised and delighted me.

"Very well! How so? I thought from what I heard you were in much pain and weakness," said I.

"Yes, sir, that is true; but I am very well for all that. For God is so good to my soul, and he provides everything needful for my body. The people in the house are very kind; and friends come to see me, and talk and pray with me. Sir, I want nothing but more grace to praise the Lord for all his goodness."

"Why, my friend, you are an old pilgrim, and I am glad to see that you have learned thankfulness as you travel through the wilderness."

"Thankfulness!" quickly returned he. "No, sir; I never did thank the Lord, I never could thank him; no, nor I never shall thank him as I ought, till I get to glory. And then—oh, then—how I will thank him for what he has done for me!" Tears of affection filled his eyes as he spoke.

"What a good Master you serve!" I added.

"Ay, sir, if the servant was but as good as the Master. But here I am, a poor old sinner, deserving nothing, and receiving everything which I need. Sir, I want nothing but more grace to serve him better. I lie here on this bed, and pray and sing by night and day. Sir, you must let me sing you my hymn; I always begin it about four o'clock in the morning, and it keeps my spirits alive all the day through."

Without waiting for my reply, he raised himself up, and in an aged and broken, but very affecting tone of voice, he sang two or three verses, expressive of God's goodness to him, and his own desire to live to God's glory. The simplicity, serenity, and heartfelt consolation, with which this venerable disciple went through it, gave a colouring to the whole, and left an impression on my mind which it would be impossible to convey to the reader.

As soon as he had finished his hymn, he said, "Do not be offended, sir, at my boldness: you love the Lord, too, I hope; and then I am sure you won't be angry to hear me praise him. But now, sir, talk to me about Jesus Christ. You are his minister, and he has sent you here to-day to see a poor unworthy soul, that does not deserve the least of his mercies. Talk to me, sir, if you please about Jesus Christ."

"Neither you nor I are able to talk of him as we ought," I answered; "and yet, if we were to hold our peace, the very stones would cry out."

"Ay, and well they might, sir, cry shame, shame upon us, if we refused to speak of his goodness," said the old man.

"Jesus Christ," I continued, "is a sure refuge, and a present help in time of trouble."

"That's right, sir; so he is."

"Jesus Christ has taken care of you, and watched over you all the days of your life; and he will be your guide and portion in death."

"That's right again, sir; so he will."

"You have committed your soul into his keeping long since, have you not?"

"About forty years ago, sir; about forty years ago, (when I first used to hear Mr. Venn and Mr. Berridge,) he came to seek and to save me, a vile sinner, who deserved nothing but his wrath. I can never praise him enough."

"Well, my friend, and this very Saviour, Jesus Christ, whom you love, and in whom you trust, lived for you, and died for you; he rose again for you, and has sanctified you by his Holy Spirit, and now lives to make daily intercession for you: and having done all this, do you think he will leave you to perish at last?"

"No, sir," said the old man: "faithful is he that hath promised, and will do it. Mine, alack, is a changing heart; but he changeth not. I believe that he hath laid up a crown of glory for me; and though the old enemy of souls sometimes tells me I shan't have it, I believe in Christ sooner than in him, and I trust I shall have it at last."

"And do you not find by experience," I added, "that his yoke is easy, and his burden light? His commandments are not grievous, are they?"

"No, sir, no: it is a man's meat and drink, if he loves the Lord, to do what he bids him."

"Where were you before you came into this infirmary?"

"In the parish workhouse of S——."

"Have you a wife?"

"She died some years since, and got to her heavenly home before me."

"Have you any children?"

"Yes, sir, I have two sons married, and settled in the world with families. One of them has been here to see me lately, and I hope he is in a good way for his own soul, and brings up his children in the fear of God."

"Have you any worldly cares upon your mind?"

"*Not one*, sir. I am come to this house, I plainly see, to end my days; for this mortification in my leg must, before it be very long, bring me to the grave. And I am quite willing, sir, to go, or to wait the Lord's own time. I want nothing, sir, but more grace to praise him." Which last words he often repeated in the course of the conversation.

"You have reason," I said, "to feel thankful that there is such a house as this for poor and sick people to be brought to, for both food, lodging, and medicine."

"That I have, indeed, sir; it is a house of mercies to me, and I am ashamed to hear how unthankful many of the patients seem to be for the benefits which the Lord provides for them here. But, poor creatures, they neither know nor love him. The Lord have mercy upon them, and show them the right way. I should never have known that good way, sir, if he had not taken compassion upon me, when I had none upon myself."

Tears ran down his aged cheeks as he spoke these last words. "Here," thought I, "is a poor man that is very rich, and a weak man that is very strong." At this moment the nurse brought in his dinner. "There, sir, you see, more and more mercies! The Lord takes care of me, and sends me plenty of food for this poor, old worn-out body."

"And yet," said I, "that poor old worn-out body will one day be renewed and become a glorified body, and live along with your soul in the presence of God for ever."

"That's right, sir," said the good old man, "so it will: 'though after my skin worms destroy this body, yet in my flesh shall I see God.' But, come, sir," seeing me look at my watch, "you must speak a word *to* your Master, if you please, as well as *for* him. I will put down my dinner while you pray with me."

I did so, the man often adding his confirmation of what I offered up by voice, gesture, and countenance, in a manner highly expressive of the agreement of his heart with the language of the prayer.

Having ended, he said, "God be with you, sir, and bless your labours to many poor souls! I hope you will come to see me again, if my life be spared. I am so glad to see those who will talk to me about Jesus Christ, and his precious salvation."

I replied, "May the God of Abraham, Isaac, and Jacob, who carried them through the days of their pilgrimage, and brought them safe to a city which hath foundations, bring you there too, and bless you all the remaining days of your journey till you get home! I am going to see several serious friends this evening, who would be glad, I know, to receive a message from one who has had so much experience of a Saviour's mercies. What shall I say to them?"

"Tell them, sir, with my Christian love and respects, that you have been to see a poor dying old man, who wants nothing at all in this world but more grace to praise the Lord with."

So ended our first interview. I could not help reflecting, as I returned homewards, that, as the object of my journey to the infirmary had been to carry instruction and consolation myself to the poor and the sick; so the poor and the sick were made instrumental to the conveying of both instruction and consolation to my own heart in a very superior degree.

I saw him four or five times afterwards, and always found him in the same happy, patient, thankful, and edifying state of mind and conversation. The last time I was with him, he said, "Sir, I long to be at my heavenly home, but I am willing to remain a traveller as long as my Lord and Master sees good."

He died [203] not long after my last sight of him, in the steadfast assurance of faith, and with a full hope of immortality.

Footnotes:

{87} The mother died not long after her daughter; and I have good reason to believe that God was merciful to her, and took her to himself.

An interesting account of a visit recently made to the Dairyman's cottage appeared in the *Christian Guardian* for October 1813. A still more recent visit to the good old Dairyman (who still lives, at the age of eighty-two) has been made by the author of this narrative. (*June* 1814)

The good old Dairyman died in 1816. His end was eminently Christian.

{97} "Now abideth faith, hope, charity, these three; but the greatest of these is charity" (1 Cor. xiii. 13)

{98} This circumstance took place before the late abolition of the slave trade.

{103} The day has since arrived, when the persevering efforts of Mr. Wilberforce to accomplish this happy purpose have been fully answered. *The slave trade is abolished.* The Church of God rejoices at this triumph of the cause of Christ over the powers of darkness.

{105} In the course of conversation, he sometimes addressed me with the word "Massa," for "Master," according to the well known habit of the Negro slaves in the West Indies; and sometimes 'Sir,' as he was taught since his arrival in England; but the former word seemed to be most familiar to him.

{107} A kind of shell-fish, which abound in the place where we were, and which stick to the rocks with exceeding great force.

{121} Song of Solomon i. 5.

{203} The foregoing conversation took place on September 22, 1808, and is faithfully related.

J— S—, the good old man, died in the Infirmary, in December 1808.

Echo Library

www.echo-library.com

Echo Library uses advanced digital print-on-demand technology to build and preserve an exciting world class collection of rare and out-of-print books, making them readily available for everyone to enjoy.

Situated just yards from Teddington Lock on the River Thames, Echo Library was founded in 2005 by Tom Cherrington, a specialist dealer in rare and antiquarian books with a passion for literature.

Please visit our website for a complete catalogue of our books, which includes foreign language titles.

The Right to Read

Echo Library actively supports the Royal National Institute of the Blind's Right to Read initiative by publishing a comprehensive range of large print and clear print titles.

Large Print titles are in 16 point Tiresias font as recommended by the RNIB.

Clear Print titles are in 13 point Tiresias font and designed for those who find standard print difficult to read.

Customer Service

If there is a serious error in the text or layout please send details to feedback@echo-library.com and we will supply a corrected copy. If there is a printing fault or the book is damaged please refer to your supplier.

Printed in the United Kingdom
by Lightning Source UK Ltd.
124740UK00001B/161/A